60

FARRAR
STRAUS
GIROUX

WHO IS LOU SCIORTINO?

WHO IS LOU SCIORTINO?

OTTAVIO CAPPELLANI

TRANSLATED FROM THE ITALIAN
BY HOWARD CURTIS

FARRAR, STRAUS AND GIROUX

NEW YORK

FARRAR, STRAUS AND GIROUX
19 Union Square West, New York 10003

Copyright © 2004 by Neri Pozza Editore, Vicenza
Translation copyright © 2007 by Howard Curtis
All rights reserved
Distributed in Canada by Douglas & McIntyre Ltd.
Printed in the United States of America
Originally published in 2004 by Neri Pozza Editore, Italy,
as *Chi è Lou Sciortino?*
Published in the United States by Farrar, Straus and Giroux
First American edition, 2007

Library of Congress Cataloging-in-Publication Data
Cappellani, Ottavio, 1969–
[Chi è Lou Sciortino? English]
Who is Lou Sciortino? / Ottavio Cappellani ; translated from the
Italian by Howard Curtis. —1st American ed.
p. cm.
ISBN-13: 978-0-374-28981-2 (pbk. : alk. paper)
ISBN-10: 0-374-28981-6 (pbk. : alk. paper)
1. Mafia—Italy—Sicily—Fiction. 2. Mafia—United States—
Fiction. I. Curtis, Howard, 1949– II. Title.

PQ4903.A55C5513 2007
853'.92—dc22

2006031304

Designed by Gretchen Achilles

www.fsgbooks.com

1 3 5 7 9 10 8 6 4 2

WHO IS LOU SCIORTINO?

He was sitting by the cast-iron stove, in the old armchair that had taken on his shape, toying with his grafting knife. Poor hopeless innocent that you were, you thought for a moment that with a thin blade like that he couldn't even stab a dog. But your grandpa could peel a man like a potato, then leave him lying there, skinned alive, reflecting on his sins.

"Better an innocent man on the inside than a guilty man on the outside," he was saying. Grandpa had been inside several times, and had never complained, he went in and out of the can like he was going to an opening at the Met, with that elegant air of his that seemed to say, *Better I take the rap than someone else . . .*

So you were still a kid when you realized that someone who'd never done time couldn't possibly be innocent, that there was no point in whining when you went in, whiners were fools, and if you made a mistake and smashed somebody's face who had nothing to do with anything, well . . . it wasn't the end of the world.

The cast-iron stove sat there waiting for you every day, warming the clothes on your back, steaming the damp out of your jacket.

And the old man tempting you, drilling it into you: You gotta get respect, but you don't boast about it, and if you gotta use force, act like you had no choice. "That's the difference between a man and a backslapper, Lou."

So you went around looking sad and fatalistic, and you gave the other kids that look, like you were saying, *One of these days, I might be forced to hurt you real bad, even if you're a good guy at heart.* And the neighborhood boys got to thinking you meant business.

Until circumstance, call it destiny, call it chance, made you mean business for real.

It was one thing to earn respect from the guys from around the way, like that *pacchiotto* Goldstein, who paid you to play in *his* pool hall. It was quite another to challenge the bosses for control.

Of course, there wasn't anything to control yet, but you knew control was what you had to have, even if you didn't yet know what the word meant. When you were kids, all you had to do was take over a bar or a pool hall and lay down the law: decide who could come in and who couldn't. Every now and then you had to smash somebody's face, just to show you could.

One day, though, they smashed *your* face . . . over some shitty little luncheonette downtown! You came home with blood caked on your lips, and the old man smiled and said, "That asshole, that fucking dickbrain"—he was repeating himself, but Grandpa liked to repeat himself—"now you gotta kill him."

He walked to his armchair, like a priest to the altar. "Oh, you don't *have* to kill him . . . You should, but it's not down to you, times are changing . . . Still, it's time you saw how the world works. See, Lou, it's a dog-eat-dog world, but once upon a time they invented something beautiful. That something's called money."

He sat down. "When they invented this thing, they thought it would help everyone to get along. But you see, the world is divided into people who can get along and people who can't. That son of a bitch didn't come to you to suggest an arrangement, he came and smashed your face. You can't do anything with people like that except kill them. Sure, it's not a pleasant thing: when you kill people like that, you gotta do it with a sad look on your face, somewhere public, so everybody can see how sad you are. *Capish?*"

You had a sudden coughing fit.

"Can't you fucking let me finish before you start puking your guts out?"

With that deadpan look he assumed on special occasions, the old man explained the meaning of control. Control meant just one thing: not paying, but getting paid, protection.

"You see, Lou, if I don't get paid protection, someone else will, and if someone else gets paid, in the end they're gonna want to get paid by me, and I couldn't stand for that. I'd have to go all up and down the neighborhood killing every last faggot who wanted me to pay. So, in order to kill the smallest possible number of people, I'm forced to make *them* pay. *Capish?*"

So Grandpa killed only the people who got in the way of his control. Then he reinvested the money, business boomed, and everyone in the neighborhood was happy. You understood, Lou, even if the FBI and the faggotass cops in the police didn't get it: they thought the money he made from control was dirty, and Grandpa couldn't make the neighborhood happy until he cleaned it off.

Now, in Los Angeles they'd invented something else: the movies. And there was a lot of money in movies. Grandpa thought it would be a good idea to make the money even cleaner.

"Forget about the luncheonettes downtown, tell that banana head who beat you up to go fuck himself, and go to Los Angeles, to our friends' film school, all right? Study hard, and maybe you won't have to kill anybody again."

You packed your bags like Grandpa told you. The morning you left, while you were trying to say goodbye to your mother, who was crying in the kitchen, your grandpa came in with good news. "You know the guy who busted your face? They lifted him ninety feet in the air on the end of a crane and dropped him on the floor of a living room paved with tiles from Caltagirone . . . There wasn't a roof on the house yet, that's why the crane was there. Now," he said, smiling, "they can't scrape the blood off because the guy's melted into the tiles."

You coughed again.

"You gave him milk, didn't you?" your grandpa said to your mother. "You shouldn't give him milk in the morning. It's bad for the stomach." Then he turned back to you. "Look, Lou," he said, "it wasn't our fault, the guy was a dickhead, he should have asked your name before he hit you, sooner or later he was going to end up on a Caltagirone floor, if it hadn't been us, it would have been somebody else . . ."

Your grandpa looked at your mother like he was hoping she'd back him up, but your mother shook her head, as if to say, *That didn't come out right* . . . so then your grandpa said, "I mean . . . if it hadn't been somebody else, it would have been us . . . how about that?" Your mother shook her head again, he still hadn't got it right, and your grandpa thought about it some more. "They're all fucking idiots . . . anyhow it wasn't us. Did you pack your bags?"

Fucking film school! The first thing they did when you got to Los Angeles was give you the books and teach you how to launder money.

The safest way was to buy or build little theaters in the suburbs all over America, hundreds of little theaters. They didn't cost much because all you needed was a garage or a Quonset hut, sometimes not even that. You bought a piece of land, put a fence around it, put up a screen with a projector and a box office, and painted the words DRIVE-IN on a wooden board. You made a few movies, showed them, and even if nobody went, you sent a courier with a briefcase full of money to buy all the tickets for a week, you paid taxes regularly on the take, the courier came back the next week, and "the fucking bacons"—that's what the guy who showed you the ropes called the cops—"can't do a fucking thing to you, because when you go to a movie nobody asks to see your ID . . . This is clean cash from decent people."

"Clean cash from decent people": the same words Leonard Trent used when he buttonholed you in your office one day a few years later.

Leonard Trent . . . that crazy cocksucker of a director who worked for Starship Pictures ("Sounds better than Sciortino Productions," your grandpa had said, with admirable modesty), the idiot who'd found out how the family was laundering money because he had a spinster cousin in Pennsylvania and because he was banging his accountant's secretary!

His cousin had gone to see his movie seven days in a row because she considered it her duty, especially since the theater was always empty . . . "It's not your fault," she said, trying to reassure her cousin the director, "it's those turds in Pennsylvania: they're so provincial, they don't give a flying fuck about art."

Leonard had moaned about it to Molly, one of his accountant's secretaries, while he was massaging her ankle, and Molly had told him, "That's impossible, your movies do very well in Pennsylvania. In fact, they do well everywhere."

"So I said to myself, either my cousin is putting me on or my movies are part of a front . . ."

When Trent buttonholed you in your office, you thought how lucky he was he'd found you behind that desk, because if your grandpa had been there instead he would have taken a gun out of the middle drawer and shot him in the forehead, just for coming in without knocking. But you wanted to be a businessman. The guy was probably planning to blackmail you, and it was the first time something like this had happened, so you were curious to see how far this dickhead wanted to go. Besides, there was plenty of time to shoot him later.

"Go on, I'm listening . . ."

"Okay. Now, you don't know my cousin, but she adores me, right? She's not married, she lives in some one-horse town in Pennsylvania because she's got nothing else to do with her life, and I'm her cousin who makes movies, right? So when my cousin finally gets me on the phone, after she's been told twenty times I'm not there (I do it for my image), and tells me, with rage and indignation in her voice, that the theater was empty seven days in a row, well, you can be sure she's telling me the goddamn truth. You follow me?"

"More or less."

"Right. Now, before you take the .22 out of the middle drawer of your desk and shoot me (because if you're going to shoot me in your office you'd better not use anything bigger than a .22 or you'll get blood on the rug and stain your jacket), just give me a fucking minute. I DON'T GIVE A FUCK where the money comes from or what the fuck you do to get it clean. I make pictures and I want my pictures to get made and all the good things that go with it: I want a good percentage of the take, and I don't give a fuck how it gets to me, or who the money belongs to. I mean, sure, now I know the money's dirty and you're using my pictures to clean it, but what the hell? Why the fuck should I care? I mean, someone else could be paying me dirty money and I wouldn't even know it. This money I happen to know is covered in shit, but so what? Am I supposed to go out looking for money that's clean? There's this kid in one of my pictures, he wears an undershirt and a leather jacket, he's got this line, 'Man, was there ever a clean dollar bill?' There sure as shit might be, but I for one haven't got the time to hunt it down, I have some pictures to make, and for the moment dirty money will do me just fine. And if you think I give a fuck, you got the wrong guy. I'm not clean, you—no offense—aren't clean, and the money that goes through this dump isn't any cleaner than we are, but just in case I haven't made myself clear, I. Do. Not. Give. A. Fuck. That's why you and I should team up and see if we can't make this fucking money even cleaner. What do you say?"

"Nothing, I'm listening."

"Right. So what I want now is to make a picture with lots of special effects, we can hire some of these young guys who are good with computers that make special effects, and we pay them salaries, then whatever the customers pay the company, they can't ask any questions, right? Because they're on salary. You own the special effects company, you're the customer, you run it the way you want, we buy the computers and all that modern shit and I make my fucking picture with special effects, except for the exploding skyscraper, I want that to be real, not done on the computer. You follow me so far?"

You nodded.

"Here's the deal with the skyscraper. The basic idea is, they want a fucking love story, I'll give them one, I'll give them one and then some. So listen. He's rich and handsome, a father figure, she's poor, she's unlucky, she's nothing much to look at now, but only because she's let herself go. The two of them meet and fall in love. Not right away, maybe twenty minutes in. Okay? Then along comes obstacle number one . . ."

"Obstacle number one?"

"Sure. First they meet, and there's your first hook—will they or won't they? But of course they will, so it's not much of a hook, just enough to keep the audience in their seats. So they meet, they fall in love, and everyone breathes a sigh of relief, *Aaahhh, that's good! They've fallen in love, I knew they were going to fall in love!* At this point, it's time for obstacle number one. Like, for instance, she runs off with his best friend, a top plastic surgeon with a clinic in South America. What a whore, you're thinking, but as it turns out, she isn't in love with the surgeon after all. Even worse, you're thinking, but no. Later we find out the surgeon's been jealous of his friend since they were children. They went to one of those schools for little assholes, you know, and the little girls always gave his friend candy but never him. So his friend ended up with all this candy the girls gave him, while he had to make do with stamps, right? So now he wants the girl. The girl herself is innocent, in fact she's clueless. What does *she* know from high society? It would never occur to her that a top plastic surgeon could have his own problems and feel such jealousy over a bunch of candy. She looks up to him. So the surgeon tricks her, he tells her if she really wants to hold on to his friend, she needs to have some work done. And obviously, he knows his friend's tastes, so he can tell her what she needs to do. So he takes her to South America, where he's got this well-equipped clinic. In the well-equipped clinic, obviously, the surgeon tries to get it on with her, but it passes right over her head, she's so intent on the man she loves, she doesn't even notice the surgeon is putting on the moves, can you see how frustrating that is for him? Here he is trying to get in her pants and she's oblivious. Okay, so now the surgeon decides to get his revenge, he operates on her and after he's operated on her he tries to rape her, to defile her. He doesn't get violent until he takes off the bandages and she says, 'Wow! I've turned out really great. I can't wait to leave here and go back to the man I love,' and she starts to pack her bags. He tries to rape her and she runs away through the streets of this South American city, since now she realizes she put herself in the wrong hands. But in the meantime the man she loves is desperate, because she didn't tell him she was going to South America, she kept it hidden because the surgeon told her his friend liked surprises, and she believed him, 'That's great,' she says, 'I like surprises, too!' and she's clapping her hands and jumping up and down, you see the kind of girl she is? So all the time they're in South America he's desperate, he thinks they've run away together and so on. He starts to drink, and I mean *drink*. And basically, he doesn't shave, doesn't change his shirt. So he's got this scraggly beard, his collar's filthy, and he walks around the streets of the city with a bottle in his hand. And the friends who meet him on the streets of this ritzy neighborhood say, 'Hey . . . hey . . .' What should we call him? Something refined. Ernest. Ernest, that's a good name for the cocksucker. So his friends meet him on the street and go, 'Ernest . . . Hey, Ernest . . .' they hardly recognize him, right? Ernest was always so elegant. 'Ernest . . .' and he looks at them like they don't exist and just keeps on walking. Then, to emphasize how he doesn't care about anything anymore, you know, I put in some gore, for instance he's walking along the street and this pet shop gets blown up by a bomb with all the customers inside. And he's walking over these little pieces of poodle without even noticing. From time to time he takes a swig from the bottle. Then he decides to end it all. He goes into his skyscraper, because he owns a skyscraper, and rides up to the top floor. Except that . . . except that just as he's about to jump he sees this taxi pull up, and who should get out but her . . . Because he isn't just rich, handsome, intelligent, and powerful, he's also got a heart of gold, so he's brought this pair of binoculars, to make sure he isn't about to flatten anybody when he jumps.

"Cut to her. She's running across this vast lobby, the lobby of the skyscraper, with her heels making, you know, a racket on the shiny marble floor, heading for the elevator. She's devastated, body and soul. She's got lips like a life preserver, a nose like a playground slide, and tits so big they look like they're going to burst. In her soul she's devastated by the things she saw in South America, the way the surgeon deceived her, how she was mistreated by the nurses, and apart from that, there was a massacre on the streets, they killed five innocent people right before her very eyes. So she can't wait for the man she loves to take her in his arms and console her. And even though she's devastated, she can't resist giving herself the once-over in the elevator mirror, you can see how heartbreaking that is, she's devastated by what she's seen, but inside she's still afraid the man she loves won't like her.

"Cut to the surgeon, brooding. He's eaten up with anger because she rejected his advances and ran away. When they first arrived in South America, the surgeon was really a very pleasant person, and kind to the switchboard operators and the people working in the clinic, so kind that she thought, *What a good man he is*, but now, after she's escaped, he changes, and loses his temper with the switchboard operators, he's consumed with anger. I forgot to mention that while he's operating on her, he's got this sinister look in his eyes, and all the women in the audience, who can see how disappointed he is, are afraid he'll kill her with the scalpel, or else scar her face, or put her nose where her mouth oughta be and vice versa. But it's just a sinister look in his eyes: when he takes off the bandages and everything's gone well, with everything in the right place, the women in the audience heave a sigh of relief . . . aaahhh. But there's still this nagging doubt. Why did the surgeon have that sinister look in his eyes if he didn't scar her? *Could it be . . . ?* In the meantime, the movie continues, are you with me?"

"Go on."

"Okay, so she's in the elevator, and we cut to the surgeon, who's brooding. And when he stops brooding, you know what he does? He sneers. That's what the surgeon does: sneers.

"Cut to the elevator. There's this catchy music in the background, catchy, but calm and relaxing. So, la la la.

"Cut to the surgeon, who's sneering and looking at an X-ray. The camera tracks in and we see the surgeon's got a remote in his hand.

"Cut to the elevator door opening. The lovers' eyes meet. They run to each other, fall into each other's arms, and kiss. Then he looks in her eyes, notices how she's changed, and says, like somebody who's found himself back in the Garden of Eden, 'Darling, I've always loved surprises.'

"Cut to the wicked surgeon, sneering, and pressing the button on the remote control.

"Cut to an exterior shot of the skyscraper, we see the top of the skyscraper explode.

"Cut to the X-ray: the wicked surgeon has filled her tits with plastic explosive! The bastard."

"Your movie is shit!"

"Spare me your fucking opinion, Lou! What are you, some cocksucker from *The New Yorker*? No. You're just a good kid who's going to build me a skyscraper. And you know why?"

"Why?"

"Because I'm going to blow the top off for my picture, and then you're going to sell what's left to a different company. For peanuts, because after all it hasn't got a top and there's not a whole lot of *market* for topless buildings, then all you have to do is rebuild the top and get yourself some tenants, and on paper your first company's lost money by underselling a skyscraper that was fine even when it didn't have a top. Your money's clean and I get to make my picture, *Plastic Love* . . . What do you think of the title?"

"It's a shit title," you said. "But the idea isn't bad . . ."

———

That was how the whole thing started.

Insane as it was, your grandfather really liked that crackpot Trent's idea. Movies, construction, and a great big fuck-you to the world!

Things were going well . . . really well . . . until one day a bomb went off in the screenwriting department. Pieces of screenwriter everywhere: they didn't know what hit them.

To keep the Feds from nosing around, officially it was a fire. Those who'd heard the blast were politely told to keep it to themselves.

Your grandfather hadn't been expecting it. Now, he said, they had to find out which motherfuckers had done such an insulting thing, and come to an agreement.

You said, "Are you telling me I gotta sit down with the people who stuck a bomb under my ass?"

Your grandfather looked at you like he didn't understand. "Lou," he said, "listen. You got a company that's right for you, no? I mean absolutely right . . . Those write-offs of yours were genius . . . So, you made a whole lot of money, and now some suckass faggot comes up to you and says, 'You know what we're gonna do? We're gonna share.' What do you do? Do you say yes? You tell him he's out of his fucking mind. Then I come and I say, 'No, let's go into business together and share.' Do you understand what I'm saying to you?"

You said nothing.

"Lou, that bomb was a smart move for those guys." He rubbed his foot—"Fucking feet are killing me!"—then said, "Listen, I'd like to see you become somebody people respect . . . like one of those guys . . . I don't know, like those fucking La Brunas from Manhattan . . . before . . . before I go . . ."

"Go where, Grandpa?"

"Nowhere. Forget about it, eh? Say"—he looked up suddenly—"do you remember Sal Scali?"

"Sal Scali? The amaretti guy? In Sicily?"

"That's right. He's got a family, he understands. Go to Sicily for a while, stay with Sal Scali."

You opened your mouth to speak, but the conversation was over.

"I don't want them to hurt you," the old man said. "Is that enough of a reason?"

It was enough of a reason. You arrived in Catania and were met by a Joe Pesci type who looked like he'd just stepped out of a Madison Avenue tailor's: Sal Scali, a guy who really put on the dog.

Pesci-Scali explained to you the genesis of the Scali Amaretti . . . how the Sicilians who emigrated to America were crazy about them, how at first they exported them in the form of cakes, how they put some dumb niggers on street corners to sell the cakes wrapped in foil, how the business grew ("Like a dick in front of Sharon Stone," he said) and how, thanks to your grandfather, Scali's Amaretti now had elegant headquarters in New York.

He revealed to you his Big New Idea: to launch Scali's Amaretti on the market packaged with little romantic mottoes. "You pick it up, you eat the amaretto, and then you read the motto to the one you love . . .

"So now," he whispered, "you're going to be . . . what do you call it? . . . a copywriter, my American copywriter, for all of Sicily, fuck it, the whole continent. We tell our friends Sal Scali's brought you over from America to write his mottoes, huh?"

He winked at you, and you knew this wasn't a man who inspired your respect . . .

But where the fuck are you now, Lou? Why is there a wad of wet cotton moving around in your head, right inside your brain? And that fucking light . . . like out-of-focus neon, like the lights in a Harlem stairwell? And this feeling of numbness in your hands? And this stench, like the smell in your uncle Alf's house on the day of his funeral?

It's dawn on an October day in Catania Civic Hospital. The young man has just opened his eyes, and can see his distorted reflection in the metal rail of his bed. He moves his feet to make sure he's alive. A toothless old man with a bowl in his hand, wearing a coarse pair of pajamas, is looking at him and smiling.

"What happened?" the young man grunts, in English, shaking himself out of his lethargy.

"Eh?"

"What happened?"

The old man goes on smiling. *"Minchia*, that's all we needed— *inglese.*"

The young man switches to Sicilian. "You know," he says in a weak voice, "I can speak Sicilian better than you."

The old man can't stop smiling, he's so happy. "Tea!" he says, pointing to the cup, with an expression in his eyes that suggests he's never drunk tea at home.

"How long have I been here?" the young man asks.

The old man doesn't answer. *Why should I tell you?* he seems to be thinking.

The young man stares at him. The old man stares back and sips his tea.

The young man shakes his head, then says, "I don't know how

long I've been in this hospital, but I do know one thing. I usually carry a gun, sometimes I put it in my shoulder holster, you know what that is, don't you? The kind you put under your armpit, it keeps the gun nice and warm. But sometimes I carry it on my holster belt . . . you know, near the back, so the handle sits right in the hollow of the kidneys. That way you can wear a tight jacket and nobody sees you got a gun. Well, not exactly nobody, because if you got a trained eye you can tell. But you couldn't tell, old man. Then there are ankle holsters, you know what I'm saying? Ankle holsters are for shit, they're uncomfortable, you walk like you got a limp, you can't cross your legs when you sit down, in other words, a waste of fucking money. You know something, old man? It's doing me a lot of good, talking to you. You really need somebody to talk to once in a while . . . Anyway, like I said, I don't know how I ended up here, I don't know who took my clothes off, I don't even know if I was dressed when they brought me here, but . . . listen carefully here . . . I *usually* pack a piece. Are you following me?"

The old man says nothing. He thinks the young man is delirious.

"Now, it may be when they take you to the hospital and take your clothes off they also take your gun away, I don't know, this is the first time I ever came into a hospital unconscious, and I don't know the rules. But do you think there's a remote possibility my clothes are in that dresser—you see that dresser?—my clothes and my gun? I doubt it, but what do *you* know? Are you sure? Of course you're not. In other words: we don't know. And that's the point: neither of us knows. Now, here's the deal. I get up, I open the dresser, and I see if my gun's there. If my gun's not there, I'll have to be patient: I'll go back to bed and find somebody else to ask. But if my gun is there, I swear on my honor I'll take it and cap you in the knee if you don't tell me right now when they brought me here. Is that a risk you want to take?"

"Yesterday afternoon."

"Yesterday afternoon. Very good."

NICK IS ON HIS WAY HOME

ick is on his way home. His face and jacket are stained with blood, he walks quickly but cautiously, his pants falling down over his hips, the hem caught under the heels of his moccasins.

He's carrying a guitar case. He feels cold, and he's just reached the street where he lives: a street of identical little villas off a busy highway. Across the highway, vacant lots, clumps of grass yellowed by the sun between dark masses of volcanic rock.

The neighborhood isn't downtown, it isn't a residential area, and it isn't a suburb: it's all of these things, depending on how the street is lit. Right now there's not much light, but there's a huge billboard advertising a company that makes wedding dresses, and his neighbor Tony's garden is all lit up for a party . . .

Nick picks up speed. He's limping. He must have sprained his ankle somewhere. He hopes nobody sees him. He walks even faster.

Tony, who's holding a huge steak impaled on a carving fork,

sees him, and his face lights up. "Nick!" he shouts. "Nick! The barbecue!"

Fucking barbecue!

Tony's face is as smooth and shiny as a baby's ("It's a gift from the Lord," he tells his customers. "It's a curse," says Uncle Sal, who thinks "a man should have a man's face"). One day he started wearing silk shirts with huge collars, soft matching scarves, and pants too narrow even for somebody with a face like his. After a while, the reason became clear: he'd opened a hairdressing salon in the neighborhood, called Tony's, a kind of catacomb furnished like an old-style bordello. ("It ought to be in San Berillo, with the hookers," Uncle Sal remarked.) When he isn't doing the neighborhood ladies' hair, he's throwing barbecues in his garden, weather permitting. Even in October, when the weather isn't too good: he's got at least four months of abstinence ahead of him and, *minchia*, he might as well put the garden to good use while he can.

Tony liked Nick from the start.

A few months earlier, he'd been worried about the house next door. It had stood vacant ever since the previous occupant, Signor Pulvirenti, left after the last of many arguments over the barbecues. Tony didn't want to find himself with a new Signor Pulvirenti as a neighbor.

The whole thing had come to a head one evening when, after the umpteenth disagreement, Signor Pulvirenti had taken aim with his garden hose and given the barbecue guests a shower. What Signor Pulvirenti didn't know was that one of the guests was Uncle Sal, who that evening was wearing a bespoke suit with a thin light-blue pinstripe he'd just had delivered from Pavone, the Neapolitan he's been using for years.

Uncle Sal likes to indulge a few "weaknesses," as he says to his friends: made-to-measure suits, strange ideas ("brainwaves," he calls them), and his niece Valentina, who's at training college, or professional something-or-other institute like they call it these days, studying to be a designer. When the spray from Signor Pulvirenti's hose scrambled the pinstripes on Uncle Sal's new suit, the barbecue plunged into a somber silence.

On the other side of the hedge, oblivious to everything, Signor Pulvirenti had continued shouting.

Dripping wet, Uncle Sal had merely opened his arms wide and smiled, like a Pope saying, *No, I won't absolve you this time, God's will be done.*

Articulating his words clearly, he'd said, "Wet new clothes, lucky new clothes," and left the barbecue. Out on the sidewalk, his driver, head carefully bowed, had opened the door of the black Mercedes.

The following day Uncle Sal had paid a visit to the party in question, and that very afternoon the party in question had moved out. When Tony discovered that the house had a new tenant, he decided to be a good neighbor and make the first overtures.

He found out that the newcomer hailed from Porto Empedocle, that he was studying at the Faculty of Agriculture, and that his name was Nick. One evening he knocked at his door and asked him The Big Question: "Nick, do you have anything against . . . barbecues? You know . . . the smoke, the smell . . . Do they— what's the word kids use these days?—you know, do they bug you?"

Nick stared at Tony's yellow shirt, orange scarf, and baby face. "Not at all."

When Tony got back home, he said to his wife, "He's a good kid, polite . . . and real good-looking!"

That was the evening Valentina, who'd come to see her cousin Tony, started to take an interest in Nick, an interest she'd never taken in anyone before.

It was also the evening Nick became a regular guest at Tony's barbecues.

"Nick, Nick!" Tony shouts again. "Come on over!"

Nick hopes the guests won't notice anything. He turns his head, counting on the fact that the lighting is in his favor, and says, walking faster, "Is that a barbecue? Gosh, I can't, Tony . . . I have to run home and make a call."

Tony stands there, with the carving fork in his hand, disappointed.

Disappointed and worried.

This is the first time Nick has turned down his invitation.

Really, the first time.

It's not like him.

Uncle Sal looks at Nick, looks at Tony, and nods with a serious expression.

When Uncle Sal nods, it's obvious he isn't thinking nice thoughts.

"That kid's too polite . . . I told you" (though he never had). Then he delivers his verdict. "He's a snob."

Meaningless words, a simple opinion, almost a cliché between relatives. But to Uncle Sal, *snob* has a particular meaning. Snob means lack of respect, contempt for tradition . . . a brazen, conscious arrogance, a sin of pride that nobody, not even the Agnus Dei, can take away from the world. To Uncle Sal, snob means the *Opposite*: the Opposite of everything that's worth living and dying for. In other words, the Opposite of the Family.

Valentina turns pale, and Tony stammers something incomprehensible.

For a brief moment, Uncle Sal hesitates, like there's a small doubt eating away at the edifice of his thoughts; then the anger returns, more concentrated than ever.

"A SNOB," he says again.

Nick reaches his front door.

"Fuck," he says, "fuckfuckfuck." Getting his keys out is a problem, it's not easy to slip his hands in the pockets of his pants, because his hands are also covered with blood. Then he says, "Fuck," again, takes the plunge, and slips his dirty hands in his pockets.

The lock yields abruptly.

Nick hurls himself inside and slams the door behind him. Without even turning on the light, he starts to undress, hopping with one leg still in his pants, gets to the washing machine, and throws everything in.

Then he frantically turns the temperature control.

Via Etnea cuts the city like a whiplash, leading straight up to the volcano. On the right as you climb, about halfway up, there's a dark back alley that links Via Etnea with Piazza Carlo Alberto. In the morning, the piazza is lively, full of merchants with their stalls. In the evening, though, it's empty and deserted, lit only by a pink, ghostly light. A few hundred yards farther down, there are pubs, nightlife, but it doesn't reach this far. A few students going home drunk, now and then. A few sudden shouts that echo and immediately die, nothing more. In the alley, the electric lights shine back from the wet sidewalks and the rivulets left by the October storm. It's the time of year when people are happy to start wearing wool sweaters in the evening.

One bar is still open. Inside, four men are sitting around a plastic table, hanging on Uncle Mimmo's every word.

Uncle Mimmo owns a general store in the neighborhood. He's always been called Uncle Mimmo, no one remembers why.

"Fuuuuuuck," Nuccio says, stifling a laugh. "I've seen some dead people, let me tell you, but that's the deadest motherfucker I ever saw."

Tuccio is at the wheel of the beat-up Mercedes. He's driving at high speed. "What the fuck you laughing about?" he says to Nuccio.

"Who? Me? I wasn't laughing," Nuccio replies indignantly. "But fuck, did you see the way his head exploded? How the fuck did he get a head like that? It burst like a balloon!" And he laughs.

Tuccio looks at him.

Tuccio isn't laughing.

In the bar, after so much has already been said, and everybody's waiting for Cosimo to say, "Closing time," Uncle Mimmo says point-blank, "If I'd told him about the crossbow, the sergeant might still be alive right now." He says it like he's expressing something that's been burning him up inside and won't give him any peace.

"A crossbow?" one of the men asks, surprised.

"What crossbow?" another of the men asks.

The conversation revives.

In his general store, Uncle Mimmo sells bars of soap, toothpaste, brooms, dusters, shoe polish, sponges, shaving foam, razor blades, bleach, and toilet fresheners, as well as every detergent on the market. He also sells a few different kinds of eau de cologne and after-shave and, of course, DDT and Flit.

Cosimo's barman Turi says the flies in Uncle Mimmo's store are such survivors because growing up with all these chemical products has made them immortal.

The store is a little less than six feet wide and a little more than six feet long. Because of the metal shelving, two customers can't be in there at the same time, one of them's got to stand aside, and the merchandise is always falling on the floor. To avoid getting up every time to put things back, if there's somebody in the store and a second customer arrives, Uncle Mimmo says, "Please wait outside, I'll serve you next."

The flies live in the section where the fabric softeners are. They form a tight black cluster that sticks to the bar holding up the metal shelf. They're all over each other, one on top of the other. Eleven and a half inches of flies, as thick as paste, but living and moving. When Uncle Mimmo gets up to check, they scatter in an instant as if they never existed. If a customer passes, though, they keep still and merge into the darkness.

No customer has ever noticed them.

They wait until there's nobody in the store; then they take off like squadrons, even though they give the impression of only ever being *one* fly, *the same* fly. If Uncle Mimmo kills one of them with his newspaper, another comes out of the corner and takes the place of its fallen comrade, perfectly imitating its flight and buzz.

In order not to fall for their tricks, Uncle Mimmo has to keep count of the corpses.

"If I'd told the sergeant about the crossbow," Uncle Mimmo goes on, "then the robber would have seen the sergeant talking to me at the cash desk and might not even have come in. There was a cross-bow under the counter."

"There was a crossbow under the counter?" a third man asks.

Uncle Mimmo looks up, slowly. "Every afternoon after lunch," he says, "I clear the table. After I clear the table, I sit in the arm-chair, in front of the TV, to get a couple hours' sleep. I always do that, you know: sit in the armchair in the afternoon, with a blanket over my knees if I'm cold, turn on the TV, and fall asleep."

The listeners nod, but they're getting impatient.

"So I can get to sleep easier, you know," Uncle Mimmo goes on, "I put on the afternoon show on Antenna Sicilia, the one with Salvo La Rosa. Sometimes they have that comedian on, you know, the funny one, but this afternoon he wasn't on, Commander Fra-galà was on."

"The one who owns the gun shop?"

"The one who sings?"

"That's the one. First he sang an aria from *L'Elisir d'amore*, then Salvo La Rosa sat him down on the guest couch and interviewed him about the new pump-action rifles, the ones he just got in. The Commander said things are great in America, you can go into a shop, take a look at what's on the shelves and in the windows, then go to the salesclerk and say, 'Wrap up this pump-action rifle for me, please,' and he wraps it up."

"It's true," Pietro, who's retired, says. "I saw it in a movie."

Uncle Mimmo makes a gesture with his hand like he's saying, *What did I tell you?* Then he nods thoughtfully. "The Commander complained to Salvo La Rosa that things in Italy aren't so easy."

"Of course they're not easy," Cosimo says, "but here we have people you can go to who'll sell you anything, even a submachine gun. The one with the Russian name."

"Oh, sure," Uncle Mimmo says. "But who the fuck goes to those people?"

They all make resigned expressions, one with his hands, one with his face, one with his legs.

"I've been thinking about that," Tano says. He's also retired, but helps out in the bar from time to time. "In my opinion, the reason they don't come to you and ask you to pay protection is because you've been in the neighborhood all your life and everyone knows you. Maybe they like you and think they'd be showing a lack of respect if they came and asked you to pay protection."

"Yes," Cosimo says, "they think they're doing us a favor. But look how things end up."

"Precisely," Uncle Mimmo says. "So then you gotta think about self-defense. But whaddaya do with no permit to carry a gun?"

"Exactly," Cosimo says indignantly.

"Anyhow, I was thinking about these things this afternoon, and I decided I had to get hold of something, anything . . . I don't know, a knife, a hammer . . . whatever, because you never know during a robbery . . . Of course, I'm not saying somebody comes in with a submachine gun, you're going to pick up a hammer, because then the guy just starts laughing, but let's say he's distracted . . . right? . . . let's say he's *distracted* . . . How can you know what might happen during a robbery, maybe one of these things will turn out useful . . . you never know."

"It's getting cool," Tano says. "Want me to lower the shutter?" Without waiting for a reply, he stands up.

He walks unsteadily, crookedly, on the sawdust that Turi, the barman, has strewn on the ground—it's more useful than a doormat because the customers never wipe their feet when they come in, and more convenient, because when it stops raining he sweeps up and everything's clean the way it was.

The noise of the shutter being lowered echoes through the whole neighborhood.

"Fuuuuuck," Nuccio says again.

The lights of evening race faster across the windshield.

Tuccio drives in silence, looking in the rearview mirror every now and then and nodding to himself.

Tano wipes his hands on his frayed pants, rolled at the waist to reveal the white lining all yellowed. He walks behind the bar, takes a bottle of Punt & Mes from the shelf, and slowly returns to the table.

"So I decided to go to the Commander's shop to see if there was anything you could get without a permit," Uncle Mimmo resumes, once Tano is back in his chair. "When I got to the shop, I went to the salesgirl and explained my situation. She took out a drawer and set it on the counter with a smile, and you know what was inside? A dummy!" he says, disgusted.

"So now you're supposed to chase away magpies or what?" Cosimo says, just as disgusted.

"Just like I said! And they make dummies with this red thing around the end of the barrel so you can't hit anyone anymore."

"They do it because of the law," Tano says. "So you can't do a robbery with a fake gun."

"Yes," Cosimo says, "some fucking law. So now robbers only use real guns."

"Precisely," Uncle Mimmo replies. "Anyhow, I had to explain it all to her from the beginning. I needed something that wasn't a real weapon but close enough, that hurt but not too much, in other words a weapon that didn't need a permit. And then she took out another drawer and set it on the counter and inside there were new guns, all kinds of guns, and so I said, '*Minchia*, signorina, what are these, more dummies?' She explained they were air guns. *Minchia*, you know, air guns, right?"

"What are you, a kid on Halloween, that we gotta give you an air gun now?" Cosimo says.

"That's exactly what I said. So then she explained these guns don't shoot those little red rubber things. Now they shoot these really hard little bullets and they're perfect replicas of guns on the market. If you want, you can buy the bullets with a metal core, but they cost more. At thirty feet, she says they make a bruise like this. So I asked her, 'And what if I buy them with the metal core?' Just then, the Commander, who'd just finished serving somebody else, came up to us and said, 'Then the bruise lasts longer. But what the fuck are you buying, Uncle Mimmo?'"

"He's used to handling real guns, not shit," Cosimo says.

"Precisely. So then I explained my situation again to the Commander, and he nodded, being an expert in these things. Then he told me I was right, and he'd find something to take care of my problem."

"That guy knows what he's talking about," Cosimo says.

"So he thought about it awhile, and he looked around, and said what I needed was a nice sling. They make them now with this thing you put around the handle to give it more explosive power, and they shoot these colored glass pellets that are very, very accurate, and at thirty feet the bruise they give you is something else."

"*Minchia*," Tano says.

"Wait. As the Commander was turning around to get the sling off the sling shelf, I saw a cardboard box with a colored drawing of a rat with these enormous fangs and a smile on its face. So I asked him, 'What's in there?' And the Commander smiled and said, '*Minchia*, Uncle Mimmo, why didn't I think of that before?'"

"It was a crossbow," Uncle Mimmo says, spreading his arms wide. "The Commander told me that officially they're used for killing rats. Though I find that hard to believe, because to kill a rat with a crossbow first you gotta corner it, and that's the hardest part with rats. Unless, like the Commander said, there are people who like trapping rats with glue to use for target practice!"

"That's disgusting!" Turi cries.

"Shut up," Cosimo says, "you don't know anything about target shooting. And then?"

"Then I went to open up the store, with this nice crossbow all wrapped up under my arm. I sat down at the cash register, I read the instruction booklet, and I put it under the counter stretched really tight and ready to go."

"Like a hard-on . . ." Turi says to regain his credibility, and indeed they all smile, except for Uncle Mimmo, whose face grows serious.

"It's no laughing matter," Uncle Mimmo says. "You see, when the sergeant came in, I wanted to tell him about the crossbow. Just to show off, you know, to tell somebody who knew from weapons. But I could just see the sergeant saying, 'Hmmm . . . let me see that crossbow, Uncle Mimmo . . . hmmm . . . don't need a permit, eh?' and then taking it away and giving it to the laboratory for analysis, and then after a few months an article coming out in the paper saying they'd made a law that you couldn't buy these crossbows anymore without a permit. What did I know? So I thought, *Better keep it to yourself.* So I just said, 'Good evening,' to the sergeant and he said, 'Good evening,' and went off into the back on the left—where the men's toiletries are. Thinking about it now, God, thinking about it now, if I'd told him about the crossbow, then maybe the robber would have seen him talking to me at the cash register and wouldn't even have come in, he'd have put off the robbery, and the sergeant would still be alive."

Uncle Mimmo shakes his head and looks down, his mournful expression reflected in his Punt & Mes.

"When it's your turn to go . . ." Cosimo says.

"*Minchia*, I don't want to think about it," Tano says. "There were pieces of the sergeant's brain dripping from the deodorant shelf and falling on his face."

"All right, all right," Cosimo says, wiping his hands on his pants. "It's late, time to go."

A few hours earlier, Uncle Mimmo had turned on the light at the exact moment when the dark outside was really dark. (The only lighting in the store is from two small naked bulbs but, due to a strange phenomenon he's never understood, they don't light anything at all when it's just starting to get dark.) The sergeant came in, as he always did at that time, and the flies stopped buzzing. Uncle Mimmo said hello, and the sergeant returned his greeting absentmindedly, and walked straight, as he always did, to men's toiletries.

With his knee, Uncle Mimmo pushed the crossbow farther into the shelf under the counter. The stool he was sitting on rose dangerously on two legs. Uncle Mimmo felt the hard wood of the shelf against his knee, a sign he couldn't push anymore, and he let himself fall back.

The stool made a sharp noise against the tiles.

The sergeant, lost in thought, heard the noise. He'd already put on his glasses to read the label on a bottle of aftershave, and was looking puzzled. Maybe he wanted to try a different brand. He poked his head out of the corner where the flies were, holding the aftershave in his hand, then disappeared again.

Uncle Mimmo relaxed.

Then the door creaked open and there was the usual rush of air that, Uncle Mimmo knows, continues even when the door is closed again and the customer comes in.

"Please wait outside, and I'll serve you next," he managed to say before turning and finding something cold and hard under his nose, and a face in front of his eyes, a face he couldn't see clearly, being farsighted. The face whispered something. Uncle Mimmo didn't understand. The face screamed, "The money, old man!" *Fuck*, Uncle Mimmo thought, *a robbery!*

He'd never been robbed before. He was seized by a sudden panic. He thought about the crossbow, the sergeant, then nothing . . . With his free hand, the robber pressed the key that opens the cash register. The register went TLING and then TA-TANG, making the whole counter shake. The sergeant, with another aftershave in his hand, heard the TA-TANG. He looked up, then peered back out of the corner with the flies. He saw what was happening. It was only a split second. He rotated one hundred and sixty degrees, simultaneously taking out his service revolver, gripping it in both hands, and removing himself from the line of fire. He lifted the gun close to his nose and his glasses, pointing upward, his elbows bent and loose but ready for the impact, his back against the wall, or rather against the shelf of the men's toiletries section. A can of shaving foam fell to the floor with a thud.

Uncle Mimmo heard, in this order: the sergeant shouting something, but too loud for him to understand what; a tremendous bang that exploded in his left ear; a buzz spreading inside his head. He opened his eyes wide as spattered pieces of the sergeant's brain hit his face.

Like almost everyone, Uncle Mimmo had seen the footage of the Kennedy assassination on TV, with all those little pieces of brain rolling across the trunk of the convertible like foam from the soap in a car wash. At that moment, in the store, absurdly, he had that scene before his eyes, and, equally absurdly, thought it was obvious the President of the United States couldn't have died with a little red dot on his forehead like the ones the Indian women put on like tattoos. And yet, or so it seemed, even a Neapolitan sergeant (but was he really Neapolitan?) wearing glasses died this way, spattering brain matter all over the place as if he were the President.

The guy who'd fired the shot must have thought something similar, because Uncle Mimmo heard him say, "Fuuuuuck!" Then he saw him run out with his rifle case in his hand and wondered how he'd managed to put the rifle back in the case so quickly, how he could be so . . . clear-headed!

"It was a fucking rifle, not a pistol, that's why he spattered!" Uncle Mimmo said in a loud voice before collapsing onto the stool.

"And if it hadn't been for that bang, I'd have recognized the son of a bitch: *minchia*, he had a face that looked like it had fallen in a baking tray and been put in the oven!" Uncle Mimmo says now on the street, raising the collar of his jacket and saying goodbye to his friends.

"WHERE'D YOU GET THIS MEAT, TONY?"

Where'd you get this meat, Tony?" At Tony's barbecue, Uncle Sal is trying to lighten the atmosphere in his own way. "I nearly choked! I told you a thousand times to buy your meat at Tano Falsaperla's, he's got family in Argentina!"

"He was closed, Uncle Sal!" Tony replies, too cheerfully. "But you've given me an idea, you know? For the next barbecue, I'll get you a nice *asado*!"

Uncle Sal smiles, pleased with himself.

The whole family is at the barbecue.

First of all, Tony's wife, Cettina, in a showy green satin dress, and Sal's three sisters: Tony and Rosy's widowed mother, Agata; Carmela, who's unmarried; and Rosaria, the mother of Alessia, Mindy, Cinzia, and Valentina, a widow but not beyond the shadow of a doubt, in the sense that her husband disappeared and his body has never been found. On the rare occasions when she talks about the missing man, Lullo Caruso, Rosaria never fails to say, "The big fat bastard!" A comment that arouses the legitimate suspicion that Sal Scali was in some way involved in Lullo's disappearance.

Then there are all the half relatives, relatives through marriage, the children of cousins who emigrated, nephews of dead uncles, husbands of cousins of brothers, grandmothers of somebody, grandmothers in black with shawls, arranged at random around the barbecue like the spots on a Dalmatian . . . And, last but not least, Alessia, Mindy, Cinzia, and Valentina Caruso.

Tony's younger sister, Rosy (about fifteen or twenty years younger, you'd say, if you knew Tony's exact age), is sitting on a wicker couch that she says is killing her stockings. She looks around anxiously.

"*Minchia*," she says to Cinzia, "let's hope Steve doesn't stop by."

"Why didn't you invite him?" Cinzia asks, trying to balance a huge plate of meat on her lap.

"What are you, stupid? Steve was supposed to be going to the opening of a pub this evening and, because of this asshole barbecue, I had to tell him I had the flu. Do you think I could have told him, 'No, I can't come because I gotta go to a barbecue given by my hairdresser brother'?"

Cinzia shakes her head in sympathy.

"And you know how well he took it. 'What,' he says, 'you gotta get the flu tonight of all nights? You want me to show up with some dog and make us both look like a couple of losers?'"

"So what did you say?"

"What did I say? What did I *say*? I slammed down the phone! Sure, the flu was a lie, but excuse me, did *he* know it was a lie? He tells me off because I got the flu? Asshole!"

Cinzia is trying to cut the meat into smaller pieces.

"How can you eat that crap?" Rosy says. "It's all . . . hacked to pieces!" She laughs. "It looks like the fly on Steve's pants."

Cinzia lifts her knife and fork from the plate.

"Steve cuts his jeans with scissors. Here!" Rosy says, putting her hands between her legs. "Then when he puts them on, he staples them!"

Cinzia says nothing.

Rosy sighs. "*Minchia* . . . let's just hope he doesn't happen to drop by!"

The black Mercedes is parked in front of Tony's garden. Tuccio, his eyes still on the wheel, says to Nuccio, "We're going to get out now and go to the fucking barbecue, and you keep your mouth shut. Got it? I'll do the talking. Let me do the talking. Make like you're not here. Got it?"

"Fuuuuuck, what a fucking kaboom!"

"I said shut up!"

"Do you realize what bullshit that is? I don't envy anybody's penis! What I've got is clearly an Oedipus complex!"

In Tony's kitchen, Alessia, who's studying psychology, is telling Mindy she's the living refutation of psychoanalysis and all that bullshit about men and the Oedipus complex, because *she's* the one who wants to kill her father!

"Ale, you haven't even got a father," Mindy says.

"So what? Makes no difference . . . I'd like to kill Uncle Sal!"

"It isn't nice to kill anybody," Mindy says.

"In my head, Mindy, don't you get it? Only in my head . . ."

Mindy is dressed in one of those dresses her mother makes her from a pattern. She looks like a figurine cut out of one of those fashion magazines that aren't really fashionable, the cheap ones that come wrapped in cellophane and offer packs of low-quality cosmetics by mail order from companies nobody's ever heard of. Her face, though, has nothing to do with her dress, it's a normal face.

Tony bursts into the kitchen, looking like someone with an

urgent need to let off steam. He stops in front of the girls and starts to drum with his foot on the floor.

"What happened, Tony?" Mindy asks.

Tony says nothing and keeps on drumming with his foot. He's acting like a sulky little kid, but not for the usual reason that the color of the paper napkins doesn't match the color of the glasses, or the fact that Cettina watered the garden only two hours before the barbecue, so now all the guests have got wet shoes, not to mention the ladies in sandals . . . It's not even because of the beer Cettina forgot to put in the fridge, even though it was right there in the kitchen, and when a housewife enters a kitchen and sees bottles of beer the day of a barbecue, then she *puts them* in the fridge. *I mean: it's something automatic, instinctive, like blinking if somebody tries to stick their finger in your eyes . . . And if a person doesn't do it, then she doesn't do it on fucking purpose!* But that's not what's making him tense. It's Uncle Sal and his fucking remark about Nick! *What was the name of that fucking antique dealer?* Tony can't remember, but he remembers perfectly what Uncle Sal said the day they found his body slashed with a razor blade. "Everybody knew the guy was a snob." *That's what he fucking said!*

Tony stops drumming with his foot.

"Valentina's looking very pale," he says. "I don't think she's feeling well . . . You'd better get out of here!"

Tuccio and Nuccio enter Tony's garden, cutting right though the guests. They don't say hello to anybody, they're looking for Uncle Sal and no one else.

Nuccio walks confidently, with a blissful look on his face like somebody thinking, *Fuck, I'm a really handsome guy and I bet these whores are getting excited. I smell pussy!* Fantasizing, Nuccio adjusts his balls.

Tuccio, on the other hand, walks fast, face drawn. He hopes he won't bump into Uncle Sal right away: he had a clear plan in his head before he got out of the Mercedes, he'd carefully weighed his words and gestures, silently mimed the right expressions, but the lights and faces at the barbecue have driven every thought from his mind.

So for the third time now, he passes the same face. *Either they're going around in circles or Tony's garden isn't as big as it seems.* Tuccio stops to look at the face, a face he knows, even if he can't remember exactly who the fuck it is. Not knowing what to do, Tuccio says good evening.

The guy says good evening, too, politely, like a rambling old man met by chance on a one-way street.

Nuccio is wondering why on earth Tuccio is talking to that fucking guy instead of Uncle Sal. But it's none of his business. He makes a little gesture with his shoulders, a little shake, like he's straightening a very well-cut jacket, though he's not wearing a well-cut jacket, then readjusts his balls. The guy facing him makes an embarrassed sign with his eyes, indicating a point behind Tuccio's back.

Tuccio doesn't understand, he'd like to say to the guy, *What are you looking at, you little faggot?* But the guy's a guest at Sal's nephew's barbecue. He may even be a Scali. So Tuccio blinks a few times as if to dispel the aggressive feelings rising inside him.

The guy repeats the gesture, and it's even more embarrassing.

Tuccio decides to turn around (he doesn't know why he decides to turn around, but he does) and sees Uncle Sal standing there, with his hands in the pockets of his dark gray worsted jacket. Tuccio thinks, *Fuck, he's pissed about something, otherwise he wouldn't have his hands in his pockets . . . a guy like that doesn't put his hands in his pockets if he isn't pissed.* Tuccio tries to approach Uncle Sal, looking as nonchalant as he can, but as he walks, his body and feet seem to be going in different directions.

Uncle Sal stands there with his hands stuck in his pockets, while Tuccio, who's quite a bit taller, bends to whisper something in his ear. The guy who was in his way, and who's watching the scene now with feigned detachment, sees for a moment in his mind's eye the grille of the confessional, an image that used to disturb his adolescence.

Uncle Sal is listening, solemn and motionless, his lips curled in a bitter grimace.

Meanwhile in New York, at the offices of Starship Pictures, in Lou Sciortino's former office to be precise, Frank Erra is sitting at Lou's former desk and rummaging nervously through the drawers.

"Chaz! Chaz!" he shouts out of the corner of his mouth, the other corner being entirely occupied by one of his usual Cohiba Coronas Especiales. "What kind of crummy office is this? They haven't even got a fucking lighter!"

Frank Erra is in Lou Sciortino's former office because, about a month ago, Lou's grandfather, Don Lou Sciortino, summoned Pippino the Oleander, Tony Collura, Jack Bufalino, and Turi Messina to his house and, pointing to the phone with a grave, solemn gesture, said, "Turi, call John La Bruna for me, please!"

Turi Messina turned white. The previous weekend, in one of the best tapas restaurants in New York, Turi Messina had met Angelo La Bruna together with two Puerto Rican girls with these breathtaking Spanish asses, and so he could flirt with those asses he'd thrown caution to the winds and started talking to Angelo, the nephew of John La Bruna, his boss's rival.

"Don Sciortino, you gotta believe me . . ." Turi stammered.

"Okay, okay, son," Don Lou said softly, "it's all right . . . it's all right. I owe you an explanation."

The explanation was that a couple of months had gone by since the bomb had exploded in their faces, and they still knew fuck all, but now they had to deal with whoever was responsible . . . "Like the Chinaman says . . . or was it somebody else? Who was it? *Minchia!* If the enemy won't come to you, you gotta go to the enemy!" Don Lou had said, getting confused between Sun-tzu and the Prophet. "Anyway, Turi, call me that suckass John La Bruna!" And Turi had called.

After the voices of a couple of secretaries, probably interrupted giving blow jobs, Turi heard the voice of John La Bruna in person and passed the receiver deferentially to Don Lou.

"How are you, John?" Don Lou said.

"Lou!" La Bruna replied. "Lou! What a nice surprise! I'm fine. How you doin'?"

"Fine!" Don Lou said.

"*Cazzarola*, Lou! What an unexpected pleasure!"

"I got a problem, John."

"Tell me, Lou," La Bruna replied sympathetically.

"I need somebody at Starship Pictures . . . Somebody who understands something about the fucking movie business."

"*Cazzarola*, Lou! I should have called you before! How can you ever forgive me? . . . Shit! The world we live in these days. Bombs going off for no reason!"

"No problem, John, no problem . . ." Don Lou replied.

"If I understand you, Lou, you need somebody to take your grandson's place."

"Exactly, John! I guess you know I sent my grandson to Sicily. To get a bit of sun!"

"You did the right thing, Lou . . . absolutely! Hmm, let me think it over a little, eh, Lou?"

"Take all the time you want, John—" Don Lou said, meaning days, weeks, or months.

"There may be somebody . . ." La Bruna interrupted. "He's still a kid . . . but he's smart . . . Do you know Frank Erra, of Erra Productions?"

"No, John, but if you tell me he's somebody you can trust, I believe you."

"Okay, Lou, let me talk to the kid, I'll call you back."

"Okay, John, talk to you later!" Don Lou said in conclusion. Then, turning to his men, "That's enough fucking around for now!"

"Chaz!" Frank Erra shouts again in Lou Sciortino's former office. "What the hell is this?" (In one of Lou Sciortino's former drawers he's just found a knife.) "Jesus! Who can you trust? What were they doing with this knife?"

Frank Erra is short (not much more than five feet tall), fat, and bald, with a rubbery neck. Right now he's wearing an elegant gray flannel suit too pale for a man of his bulk, but only six years before he was a waiter at the Sarago, a restaurant where every evening they sang *Autunno, Maruzzella, Cristo è o paese d'o sole*, and where the prominent customers were Vicienzo Arpaia, Carmine Quagliarulo, Benny Gravagnuolo, and, of course, John La Bruna. Later he became the manager, and that meant keeping the books. Frank was very careful about keeping the books. He had a healthy terror of the books not balancing, and that terror has taken him far. When everybody threw themselves into movies because there was a lot of money to be made, and you needed companies that spent a lot to launder it, Frank became the figurehead for the La Brunas' company. Erra Productions had a beautiful, spacious office in Manhattan, with a huge white leather couch Frank used for banging young actresses who wanted to hit the big time. He didn't have much influence, but he always managed to get them a walk-on.

When they put him in charge of the Sciortinos' Starship Pictures, Frank was really touched, the way his nephew Al had been the day Frank lovingly showed him how a gun was made. He was only a figurehead, his name meant less than nothing in New York. But they knew that, even if he didn't count for shit, he was practically one of them. *Madonna*, they'd put *him*, not illustrious sons and nephews like Angelo La Bruna or Alphonse Quagliarulo, at the head of a business that took real balls. Frank would have liked to get to know one of these sons or nephews who'd been pushed aside to make way for him, and show him his office and sit him down there, at *his* desk, and say, "Don't worry about it, kid, everybody in the family has his place according to his abilities, and that's why I'm here and you're doing something else, but if you want to come here and sit in this armchair behind this desk you can do it whenever you like, because Frank Erra is someone who knows the meaning of gratitude."

Frank gets up from the desk and waddles to the door, the seat of his pants caught between his buttocks. "Chaz!" he calls again. "CHAZ! Come here!"

Chaz is his bodyguard. But he's also his confidant. Chaz listens to his stories and nods. When Chaz nods, it means his stories are okay. A good kid, Chaz. Doesn't say much, just nods.

"Come on in, Chaz. I got something to tell you."

Chaz comes in, sits down on the other side of the desk, rummages in his pockets, takes out the lighter, lights Frank's Cohiba, then nods and listens in silence.

"He *phoned* me!" Frank says. "In person, *capish*, Chaz? 'Frank,' he said, 'we've never spoken on the phone, but I know you're a smart kid, Frank, because that's what they all tell me.' I was shitting my pants, Chaz, so I stammered, 'But . . . who is this?' And he said, 'Who is this?' and started laughing, an affectionate laugh, *capish*, Chaz? 'Who is this? he asks me,' and he laughed happily. 'You want to know who this is, Frank?' he said. 'This is John La Bruna.'"

"Shit," Chaz says.

"'Book a flight to Sicily, kid,' he told me. 'Go to Catania, a friend of ours wants to meet you.' 'Please, Don La Bruna,' I said, still shitting my pants. 'May I know . . . the name of this friend?' 'You gotta know, Frank,' he said. 'His name is Sal Scali . . . he's a well-dressed guy like you, and just like you, he handles business for us. *Capito*, kid?'"

"Okay, Frank," Chaz says without nodding, "I'll go tell Jasmine to book—"

"Where the fuck are you going, Chaz?" Frank cries, nervous because Chaz hasn't nodded. "You think I can land in Catania, just like that?"

He stands up and, after a couple of attempts to unjam his pants from between his buttocks, continues, "If Jasmine makes that fucking call, I'll find myself at Catania Airport with those FBI pigs all over me! *Cazzarola!* Frank Erra plus Sicily equals disaster."

"You're right, Frank, I'm sorry . . ." Chaz says, nodding.

"We need an excuse."

"An excuse, Frank?"

"Yes, I gotta find an excuse to go to Rome."

"To Rome?!"

"Of course, Chaz, I can't go directly to Sicily, not even with an excuse, because, excuse or no excuse, the FBI will be suspicious . . . I gotta find an excuse to go to Rome, and then *from there* I gotta find an excuse to go to Sicily."

Chaz doesn't understand shit, but he nods repeatedly. And Frank, seized by a sudden wave of affection, has to restrain himself from giving him a big, passionate hug.

IT'S ELEVEN O'CLOCK WHEN NICK
GETS UP WITH A START

t's eleven o'clock when Nick gets up with a start from the armchair where he's spent the night. The TV is still on, with the
volume turned down. There's a cooking show on. There's a
huge turkey and a guy, who's also huge, in a white chef's jacket,
talking to a blonde who seems to find what he's saying very funny.
The turkey is covered in aspic, and it's so shiny, and so obscene with
its hacked-off legs and naked skin, that Nick runs to the bathroom.
In the bathroom he shivers from the cold, but still he turns on the
cold water, puts his head under the faucet, looks at himself in the
mirror, and groans.

Out of the same compulsive need that makes us go to the toilet
before we enter an operating room or after a doctor has told us
we're done for, Nick picks up the shaving foam and shakes the can.
The can slips from his hand, he bends down to pick it up, feels
dizzy, leans on the sink, looks up, fills his hand with shaving foam,
smears it on his face, shaves, and tries to whistle.

In the kitchen, he opens the fridge and is lost in wonder at the
big cartons of milk. *Why do I buy all this fucking milk? Why?* One

day he told Tony about his craving for cartons of milk. Tony nodded sympathetically. "Of course, Nick! There was that kid from that family, what was his name, the one where the father had a knot in his tie as big as an apple, and the kid with that fucking cap who seemed like the only grown-up in that crazy house, every time the family pissed him off he went to the kitchen, opened the fridge, took out this carton that was bigger than he was, poured himself a big glass, and started reflecting on life with a big milk mustache. Of course, Nick, I know all about those cartons."

Christ, Nick thinks as he pours the milk into a glass that's yellow with lime, *the fucking things that come into Tony's mind . . .*

Meanwhile the doorbell rings, three or four times, the fucking bell Nick never hears. Nick comes out of the kitchen, with the glass in his hand, turns off the TV, takes out a Charlie Parker CD, opens the stereo, slips in the CD, presses play, and sits down in the armchair again. Charlie's band starts up, hundreds of soloists playing as one. Then the band stops abruptly, waiting for Charlie and . . . Nick hears the ringing. *Fuck, there's somebody at the door!* He runs to the bathroom. His clothes are hanging on the rack. *How the fuck did I get them on the rack? Fuck it, they seem clean. The case! Where's the case?* He runs back to the armchair, the guitar case is still propped against it. Near the handle, there are shiny stains of a more opaque, darker black. The doorbell rings again. He goes back to the kitchen, takes a paper towel, wets it, rushes to the armchair, grabs the guitar case, and wipes the handle with the paper towel. The stains are still blacker than the black of the handle. He slips the paper towel in the pocket of his jeans and, heart pounding like it's part of Charlie Parker's rhythm section, reaches the door, looks through the peephole, and sees the serious, bored face of Uncle Sal. Nick opens, trying to appear normal.

Uncle Sal is looking at a point somewhere on the street that Nick can't see. He turns with a smile.

"Hello, Nick, I hope I'm not disturbing you." He comes in without waiting for an answer. "Just got up, did you? Maybe you were having breakfast . . ."

What the fuck is Tony's uncle doing here? Nick must have seen him dozens of times at Tony's barbecues. A few polite greetings, the feeling he'd met a Joe Pesci type, the real thing, not a fake like the American actor, who plays a man of honor in movies only, nothing more.

"If it's about last night's barbecue, Don Scali," Nick says, "I was just thinking of going to Tony to apologize . . ."

"You're a good kid, Nick, a real good kid . . . You can go later, Tony'll still be home. At this hour, he sends his boys to the salon: you know, those two faggots from Caltagirone. But . . . can I sit down?" Uncle Sal asks, and, again without waiting for a reply, takes out his handkerchief, dusts the armchair with a dramatic gesture, and sits. Nick hurriedly picks up the guitar case and props it against the wall where the stereo is.

"Jazz . . ." Uncle Sal says, indicating the stereo. "I once read an article about jazz by this guy in the *Giornale di Sicilia* . . . He said jazz is like . . . how do they say? . . . like coitus interruptus. They start a tune and it never ends. But I don't agree. I like it . . ."

"I'm sorry, Don Scali," Nick says. "I'll turn down the volume."

"Tony's right, you know. He always talks fondly about you, says you're a real good kid, nice manners."

"Tony's too good to me," Nick says.

Uncle Sal opens his arms like he's saying, *You're right, too!* Then he says, "So, d'you listen to the radio this morning, Nick?"

"The radio? I'm sorry, Don Scali, but—"

"I know," Uncle Sal says. "Only people who were born before the war listen to the radio in the morning . . .

"Anyway," he adds, dusting his left elbow with the fingertips of his right hand, "last night there was a murder right here . . . in the neighborhood . . . A sergeant of the *carabinieri* got whacked."

Nick's face turns red like he's been slapped in the face.

"It makes my blood boil, too," Uncle Sal says, looking into his eyes. "I mean . . . in my nephew Tony's neighborhood, a son of a bitch comes into Uncle Mimmo's store, robs a poor old man, and mows down a sergeant. It's a slap in the face, Nick, see what I'm saying?"

Trying hard to recover his composure, Nick nods.

"This morning," Uncle Sal continues, "I immediately phoned some friends of mine, *capish*? To find out more. I mean, you gotta know what happens in your own neighborhood, am I wrong? Apparently, the sergeant was shot in the mouth, in the mouth, *capish*? I mean: it's not like they know exactly what happened, because of the condition of the face, but on the shelves behind him, along with his brain they found these really tiny pieces of teeth, and from that the forensic people worked out the bullet hit him in the mouth . . . The things forensics can do these days!"

Nick squeezes the paper towel in his pocket, and realizes it's even wetter than before.

"Who's playing?" Uncle Sal says, frowning. "Duke Ellington?"

"No, Don Scali," Nick says in a thin voice. "It's . . . Charlie Parker."

"You know, Nick, I'm an old man now . . ." Uncle Sal says. "I can remember the fifties, goombahs coming over from America, talking about the Duke. *Minchia*, I thought he was a boss of bosses, but he was a musician!

"Anyway"—he looks at his watch, gets up very slowly, and just as slowly heads for the door—"it's getting late."

A few steps from the door, he stops and slaps Nick on the back. "It was a pleasure talking to you, Nick." Then, lifting the flap of his jacket near the buttons, "Tony, Tony, all these barbecues of his aren't so good for the figure . . ."

At the door, he suddenly stops. "Oh, Nick, I almost forgot, you need to be careful . . . Apparently the son of a bitch who did the robbery is someone who lives in this neighborhood . . . in this neighborhood, *capish*? It's an outrage!"

With one foot almost out the door, he stops again. "I almost forgot something else, *minchia*, I'm really getting old . . . Mindy asked me to say hello."

"Mi-Mindy?"

"Look at him, he's got a stutter!" Uncle Sal says, squeezing Nick's right cheek hard between the index finger and middle finger of his left hand. "You're pretending you don't remember, huh? Tony's right, you're a real good kid. And like all good kids, you're shy. Mindy, yes, Mindy . . . Look, we see these things, we know how these things are between you young people . . . We talk about other things, it seems like we don't notice, but we got our eyes on you! All you did last night was talk, I know . . . But you and Mindy were really hitting it off!"

"Last night?"

"Sure, last night, at the barbecue. We all saw it . . . you know what I'm saying? It's obvious you're a smart kid, like Tony says . . . Last night at the barbecue, we all saw the way you and Mindy were looking at each other . . . all of us . . . And you know what? I'm telling you this in confidence, man to man: Mindy told her mother she thinks you got a pretty face . . . *Capish*, Nick?"

Outside the door, Uncle Sal looks quickly at the street, then strokes Nick's cheek and says in conclusion, "Make sure you don't miss the next barbecue, eh, Nicky?"

ister Ceccaroli for you."

Jasmine's shrill little voice interrupts Frank's fantasizing. He's been thinking about his meeting with Sal Scali and wondering why John La Bruna said, "He's a well-dressed guy, just like you." For the first time, the words seem off-key, out of place; it hurts his feelings. "He's a well-dressed guy, just like you." *What the fuck is that supposed to mean?* "Who's he?" he replies absently.

"Mister Ce-cca-ro-li from Rome," Jasmine repeats irritably.

Frank hasn't even had time to say okay when Ceccaroli's Italianized English rings out at the other end of the line. "*Nice-a to ear you!*"

"Ceccarò," Frank says. "Let's talk Italian, huh?"

Marco Ceccaroli owns a private TV station in Rome, buys and sells almost all the TV movies made by Erra Productions, and phones Frank every week with his latest *gret ideeas* for unlikely miniseries to export to America. Frank, who doesn't give a fuck about miniseries, or maxi-series for that matter, listens to him because he buys his TV movies, but mainly because he can't say to him, "Look, it's got nothing to do with me, I'm just a name on the office door."

Until now, Ceccaroli has always talked to Frank in English, and Frank's unexpected request to talk in Italian paralyzes him. *How should I talk to him? What should I say?* he's thinking.

"Whatever . . . whatever you like, Frank," Ceccaroli stammers, trusting in Providence.

"Ceccarò," Frank says, "you know that guy in Florence who picked up Italian rights in Leonard Trent's *Tenors?*"

"I seen him a few times, Frank," Ceccaroli says, though he doesn't know him at all.

"The movie's crap," Frank continues. "It's about a tenor who nobody knows but, according to that asshole Trent, he's got 'the highest singing voice' that ever existed."

"As a director, Trent's a little eccentric," Ceccaroli says. He's a fan of Trent, and likes nothing better than talking about movies. Christ! Movies! The kind that, when you show them on TV, you know they're real movies because they don't fill the whole screen!

"I say he's an asshole," Frank says. "But anyhow . . . you know that movie was made by Starship Pictures, right, Ceccarò?"

"Sure . . . sure, Frank."

"And you know I'm in charge of Starship Pictures now . . ."

"Sure, Frank! Everybody knows that!"

"Anyhow, Ceccarò, we need to do something for the fucking movie in Italy!"

"Sure, sure, Frank, I understand," Ceccaroli says, then adds timidly, "And what do the people in Florence say?"

"Ceccarò," Frank says angrily, "they buy and then they don't do shit!"

"Frank," Ceccaroli hastens to say, "send me the cans with the trailer and I can start putting out a couple TV spots a day!"

"That's fine, but we need something . . . something . . ."

"More aggressive?" Ceccaroli suggests.

"Right," Frank says. "Anyway, Ceccarò, I want you to organize a nice premiere in Rome with journalists and critics!"

"*You ken relex-a, Frank!*" Ceccaroli bursts out: it's a Freudian slip, his hands are shaking with anxiety. "I'll rent a multiplex, send out invitations, organize a nice dinner with you and Leonard—"

"Good, good, Ceccarò," Frank interrupts. "Let's see, when's the best time to do it . . ." He leafs loudly through his diary. "*Cazzarola*, too many meetings, what a fucking life . . . Let's see . . ."

Ceccaroli's hands are shaking even more.

"So . . . I could be in Italy . . . Let's say . . . Tuesday of next week."

"Tuesday? Of next week?"

"Is that too soon?"

"No!" Ceccaroli says, but even the receiver has started shaking. "No problem! In fact, it's a great idea! A sneak preview! . . . Journalists eat them up!"

"Good for them," Frank says. "I'll have Miss Zimmermann call you. She's a ballbreaker but she's the only one here who knows what the fuck trailers are, shit like that! 'Bye, Ceccarò!"

"'Bye, Frank, and . . . thanks!" Ceccaroli says.

Frank puts down the phone, picks up a sheet of paper, writes on it, and then calls Jasmine on the intercom.

Jasmine—Jasmine Artiaco, a dyed blonde with a low-slung ass whom Frank puts up with only because she's Anthony Artiaco's daughter—arrives breathless.

"Call this number," Frank says. "I want you to arrange a trip to Italy."

"You're going to Italy?"

Frank looks at her.

Jasmine lowers her eyes to the notepad and starts to scribble.

"I've written it all down," Frank continues. "Destination, timetable, date. The only thing missing is the number of people, but I'll tell you in a couple hours. Now get Leonard on the phone."

"Leonard who?"

"Leonard . . . you know . . ." Frank says irritably.

"Leonard Trent?" Jasmine cries in excitement. "Who made *Tenors* and *Plastic Love*?"

"Chaz!" Frank cries.

Jasmine jumps. Chaz rushes in.

"She's wasting time," Frank says, pointing to Jasmine with an absentminded gesture.

Chaz, who, unknown to Frank, fucked Jasmine during their early days at Starship Pictures, looks at Jasmine as if to say, *What can you do?*

Jasmine runs out in a huff.

ncle Sal came to see you?! When was this?"

"Fifteen minutes ago, Tony . . . I already told you!"

Tony's talking to Nick, who came running straight to his house. Tony also spent a sleepless night, watching a TV auction where the presenter was getting really excited about some paintings by Cascella and Purificato. *Minchia*, Tony's got Cascellas and Purificatos in the living room, and even Carusos, just above the orange leather couch where he's stuck with Nick! But he doesn't get excited looking at them. He knows they're out of date.

"Cettina, Cettina, come here!" Tony shouts toward the bedroom. Cettina appears, half asleep, hair tousled, wearing a dressing gown like Aunt Carmela's. *Fuck*, Tony thinks, *I married a hooker!*

"Did you hear?" Tony says, trying to dismiss the bitter thought from his mind. "Uncle Sal went to see Nick!"

"When?" Cettina asks in a tired voice.

"This morning, fuck me!" Tony replies irritably. Then, turning to Nick, "And what did Uncle Sal want?"

"I don't know, Tony," Nick says. "I really don't know . . . He told me . . . he told me there was a robbery last night . . . here in the neighborhood . . ."

"A robbery! Here, in the neighborhood?!"

"Yes, a robbery," Nick goes on. "Uncle Sal says . . . somebody from the neighborhood came into Uncle Mimmo's store, robbed . . . Uncle Mimmo and shot a sergeant."

"Somebody from the neighborhood?" Tony says, eyes wide.

"Yes," Nick says, bowing his head slightly.

"Impossible!" Tony says.

"Want me to make coffee, Tony?" Cettina says.

"Okay," Tony says, "make coffee, but hey? Put some clothes on, will you?"

Cettina looks at him, alarmed, then looks at Nick with an expression of patient resignation and heads for the kitchen.

"Did you see the way she dresses?" Tony says.

Nick looks in embarrassment at the window and the view of the garden.

"But you know, Nick," Tony continues, crossing his legs to reveal the cardinal-red socks under the cuffs of his purple pants, "you know what happens to somebody in this neighborhood who does a robbery and shoots a sergeant? I mean: to you it may seem normal, I don't know, like on TV, in *Baretta*, a guy wakes up in the morning, puts on his jumpsuit, takes his gun from the gun drawer . . . *Minchia*, you ever notice something? In those TV shows, they never lock that fucking drawer. There are guns in there, and gold bracelets and necklaces, and wads as thick as this in gold money clips, it makes you think, if some deadbeat nigger has got so much money and so many gold things in that fucking gun drawer, what does he gotta do another robbery for? But the *babbasunazzo* goes out, takes a look around the neighborhood, finds a liquor store, goes in, whacks a couple of cops and the store owner, who's black like him, grabs the money, and takes off, singing like Michael Jackson! Fuck, somebody like that in Catania, they'd shoot the guy as soon as he went out the door!"

Nick is still looking toward the window.

"You see that fucking barbecue, Nick?" Tony says. "Nice, huh? It's just like one I saw in an issue of *Cosmopolitan*. You know how long it took me to get a permit to build it, Nick?"

Nick makes a face that says, *How long?*

"*Minchia*, three years! And I'm a member of the Scali family, *capish*, Nick? There's a whole bureaucracy here . . . You want to rob somebody in Catania, first you gotta find out if they're paying protection, because if they're paying protection you can't rob them, or else what's the point in paying protection? So you gotta put yourself on the list . . . I mean, if you gotta do a robbery, you gotta rob the people who don't pay protection, that way the others see those people got robbed and they start paying protection, *capish*? The organization tells you which stores you can rob and which you can't and, to avoid two people showing up at the same store to do the same robbery, the organization has to make up a fucking *schedule* . . . It's not like America here, Nick, we got no free trade!"

Tony lights one of his menthol cigarettes (he smokes exactly three a day), then continues. "Anyhow, once you got permission to do your robbery, you know, I mean *you know*, that sergeants don't get whacked, because if you whack a sergeant the cops get really pissed off . . . they never get pissed off except if some cop gets whacked, but a sergeant, can you imagine, fuck!

"When Alfio . . . you know who Alfio is? No, you wouldn't know, you weren't living here then . . . Anyhow, there was this guy Alfio who does a robbery, all authorized, papers in order. During the robbery a cop comes in, right? Now, when something like that happens, everybody knows what you gotta do is say, 'I'm sorry, Mr.

Policeman, it's true I was doing a robbery, I understand you gotta arrest me, I know it's your job, let's just try to cooperate and no one gets hurt, here's my gun, and here am I.' And the gun, Nick, is *always* unloaded, if you want to do a robbery in this neighborhood, you know, it's a rule that the gun *isn't loaded*, I mean, *cazzo*, it's a fucking rule, that way nobody fucks things up for anybody else. *Capito?* The guy does a few days in jail, and then they let him go because the jail on Piazza Lanza is overcrowded, so what are they going to do, keep people inside who do robberies with unloaded guns? The only place you can do a robbery with a loaded gun is a bank, but that's a whole 'nother story, because the protection thing's a whole lot more complicated. But if you're talking about stores, forget about loaded guns and forget about dead sergeants. *Capito?*"

"What about Alfio?" Nick says.

"Oh, yes . . . Alfio . . . So, Alfio goes to do his robbery, his gun's not loaded, right? He robs a hardware store. The guy in the store's an idiot, he thinks to himself, *I sell hardware, what the fuck can they do to me, they can burn my store down, but the store isn't mine, I rent it, and hardware doesn't burn.* You see what a dickhead he was? Anyway, what happens is, during the robbery, in walks this cop. Up to now everything's fine, the dipshit hardware guy's smiling, which is fine, let him laugh, then slip the bomb up his ass . . . Alfio gives the cop the gun, you following me? Then suddenly . . . who the fuck knows what went through Alfio's head, million-dollar question . . . suddenly he just loses it, picks up a fucking hoe, and goes and smashes the head of that poor cop, who's only doing his duty. *Capito?* The cop already put his gun back in his holster, he was just about to slap on the cuffs. Everybody in the neighborhood knew Alfio, he was a professional, that was how he made his living, he wasn't your usual misfit, he was all square with the bureaucracy, and suddenly he just goes crazy."

"And then?" Nick says.

"Then . . . then Alfio takes off. The other cop, who stayed in the car, sees something strange happening: Alfio taking off, he's never seen anything like that, he starts the car, but then he's stuck in traffic, so he gets out of the car, but by this time Alfio's gone. Let me tell you, it was a mess. Newspapers, TV reporters, street demonstrations against protection, the police pissed off, and Alfio gone. *Capito?*"

Nick nods.

"Anyway, after a few days, this cop who's in the porter's lodge just inside the entrance to police headquarters goes out to stretch his legs and sees a guy sitting on an iron bench. The guy's sitting still, with his legs crossed, and a newspaper next to him, like he's going to read it, see what I'm saying? Only the guy don't got no head, I mean, he really don't got no head. At first the cop thinks he's seeing things, he rubs his eyes, then he crosses the street and as soon as he's crossed it he realizes he wasn't seeing things: there's a guy sitting on a bench with his legs crossed, and a newspaper next to him, and no head. He runs back into police headquarters, gives the alarm, and the cops all run out onto the square, the scientific guy arrives and under the newspaper there's a piece of paper that says: HE LOST HIS HEAD SO WE KEPT IT. And that's how Uncle Sal got respect and took the place of the guy who was there before him. *Capish?* That other guy couldn't keep an eye on his *picciotti*, his foot soldiers, but Uncle Sal, fuck, yes. With him around, nobody gets out of line!"

"Uncle . . . Uncle Sal?" Nick says, looking pale.

"Uncle Sal," Tony says, looking toward the kitchen. Then he shouts, "Hurry up, Cettina! How long does it take to make a fucking cup of coffee?"

Cettina appears immediately in the living room, all dolled up in a black skirt and high heels, with a tray in her hand and a sulky expression on her face.

"How many sugars, Nick?" she says.

"Two, please," Nick says.

Tony smiles and takes his coffee without sugar. As Cettina sits, trying to pull her skirt down, he says, "So Uncle Sal came just to tell you there was a robbery?" Tony says it casually, but while he's saying it he's thinking, *I'm sure Uncle Sal came to his house to tell him he's a fucking snob.*

"He told me something else, too . . ."

"Yeah?" Tony says, lighting his second menthol cigarette of the day.

"He told me . . . everybody saw me at your barbecue last night . . . talking to Mindy . . ."

Tony looks at Cettina, who looks back at Tony wide-eyed.

"At the barbecue?" Tony says. "Last night?!"

"Yes," Nick says.

Tony stands up, shakes his leg to straighten the crease in his pants, and takes a few steps around the room, thinking, *Fuck, last night he calls him a snob in front of everybody, and this morning he goes and tells him what he tells him . . . Either Nick is done for . . . like the antique dealer . . . or Alfio . . . or else Uncle Sal has lost his shit!*

"Tell me, Nick, is there anything Uncle Sal needs to forgive you for?"

"Me? No . . . I really don't know . . ." says Nick, turning pale.

Tony makes a face, like he's saying, *I'm looking away now, I'm listening . . . I don't know . . . to the birds twittering in the garden, I'm distracted, I'm thinking my own thoughts, then I turn around, and you tell me if there's anything you need to be forgiven for.*

"I really don't know," Nick continues, "I really don't. I mean, I didn't go to your barbecue last night . . . but I don't think . . . Could it be . . . I don't know . . . could it be Uncle Sal mistook me for somebody else?"

"You know something, Nick?" Tony says, forgetting about the twittering birds or any desire he might have to understand what the fuck's going on in front of Cettina. "You're right. Uncle Sal mistook you for somebody else, he realized he made a mistake, and now he wants to forgive you . . . He always does that when he makes a mistake: first he forgives you, then he makes you part of the family."

"Part of the family?"

"Sure, part of the family . . . Mindy, right?"

"Mindy's a nice girl, Nick," Cettina says.

"Too nice, if you ask me," Tony says. "*Cazzo*, she's like Aunt Carmela!"

"Don't talk like that, Tony!" Cettina says.

"Why? Because Nick's here?" Tony says. "But Nick's gotta know about our family problems! *Minchia*, Uncle Sal's worried . . . We already got one old maid, and people have started saying the Scali women aren't the marrying kind. You know what that means, Nick?"

Nick makes a face, like he doesn't know what it means.

"Fuck," Tony continues, "if women aren't the marrying kind, it means they don't want a family, they weren't brought up with any family feeling . . . But you know something, Nick? I'm really pleased Sal talked to you about Mindy. Valentina won't like it, but at least we won't have another Aunt Carmela in the family!"

Nick makes a face, like someone who's lost the thread.

"Somebody just has to mention your name and Valentina goes all red, like she just got slapped in the face!" Tony says. He goes up to Nick, smiling, and pinches his cheeks. "Nicky, Nicky, you're a real good kid . . . innocent, but a good kid . . . Fuck, it's getting late! Let's go, I'll see you to the door."

"Thanks for the coffee, Cettina," Nick says, standing up.

"Don't mention it, Nick," Cettina says, pulling her skirt down again.

Tony would like to put his arm around Nick's shoulders, but, seeing that Nick is quite a bit taller, he decides he'll just squeeze his left forearm as they walk to the door. When they get there, Tony squeezes harder. Nick turns.

"Nick," Tony says. "You know, don't laugh at this, but I've gotten fond of you . . . Is there anything you want to tell me? I'm here for you!"

"Nothing, Tony, believe me," Nick says. "Nothing important."

"Okay," Tony says, giving him a pat on the right cheek. "You go on home."

FRANK TWIDDLES HIS THUMBS
AND LOOKS AT THEM

Frank twiddles his thumbs and looks at them, thinking aloud to Chaz. "You know what's crazy? Somebody like me who pays taxes can't go to Sicily when he wants to! I gotta justify myself to the fucking FBI!"

"We need something, Frank," Chaz says. "Just one thing, then the lawyer can say, 'Erra went to Sicily for this, that, and the other, and you know what the FBI did? They followed him, they wasted public money persecuting an honest Italian-American citizen just because of his heritage!'"

"*Madonna!*" Frank says. "These fucking Cuban cigars! Look how yellow my fingers are! Yes, Chaz, but it's got to be something plausible, otherwise the average American gets pissed off. You gotta give the average American a serious reason, not serious *to you*, serious *to him*. Because otherwise he starts to go *hmmm*, and when the average American goes *hmmm*, it means you've pissed him off. If you don't want to make him suspicious, either you're going somewhere on business or you're going to get laid! Fuck, you ever see them in the morning? You ever see one of those assholes putting his fishing rod in his car, or his tennis rackets? Bye-bye, have a nice match today, right? A nice match, my ass! They're going to get some pussy!"

"You're right, Frank, you're right . . ." Chaz nods. Then he takes a magazine from the table and starts leafing through it.

Fuck it, I could ask Greta . . . Frank thinks. *If I feel like getting blackmailed by the bitch all the rest of my fucking days.* Frank rubs his hands and looks at Chaz. "Chaz, listen . . ."

"What, Frank?"

"Listen, Chaz . . ."

"I'm listening, Frank."

"Did you ever . . . did you ever kill a woman?"

Chaz nods, still leafing through the magazine.

Frank looks at him. He doesn't know what to say. "You killed a woman?"

Chaz raises his eyes from the magazine and looks at Frank with a face that says, *Sure I did, so what?*

"Nothing, nothing," Frank says. "Just curious."

Chaz nods, and keeps on leafing through the magazine.

Frank thinks, *Fuck it, if I ask Greta to do me a favor and then get Chaz to kill her, they'll be all over me!*

The intercom buzzes.

"Hello?"

"Mr. Trent is here," Jasmine squawks.

"Send him in!"

Chaz looks at Frank. Frank winks at him. Chaz is on the alert. The door bursts open, and Leonard Trent appears, wearing a blue suit, blue shirt, and blue tie. He stands in the doorway. He looks at Frank. He looks at Chaz. He opens his arms wide.

"For once a fucking producer with a bodyguard," he says. "Shit! I'll sit here, with my back turned to the bodyguard. But you'd better look at me!

"For once," he continues, walking to the chair, "Starship gives me a premiere! You know I'm the one who put this show on the road, don't you? You know who had the idea of going into the fucking construction? Me. No one but me. And you know what the fucking Sciortinos did? They didn't even say thank you, not even so much as thank you!"

He sits down, crosses his legs, and says nothing.

Frank looks at him.

Chaz looks at him.

Leonard looks at both of them.

"You're Frank, aren't you?" he says. "Erra, right? Good. Frank Erra, I've already realized you're not like that cocksucker Lou Sciortino. Just think, he used to phone me in the morning and ask, 'Leonard, when are you going to show me the new concept?' I'd have the concept right there, on the white wrought-iron table next to the pool, but you know what I'd tell him? 'I'm working on it,' just like that . . . But you, with this premiere thing, you know what you did? You touched me, Frank, you really touched me . . ."

Chaz looks at Frank, with a look on his face that says, *Should I shoot the backslapping motherfucker now?*

Frank, though, is thinking, *The little shit wants me to ask him about his fucking concept. I'll ask him . . . you're fucking right I'll ask him!*

"You got a new concept to show me, Leonard?"

"I didn't bring it in, Frank. You know, I hate people who walk around with a pile of papers. But if you want, I can give you the basic pitch."

"Pitch me, Leonard," Frank says, looking at Chaz, who turns away in disgust.

"Okay, Frank, so there's this guy who's an architect. But he's not just any architect. He builds Gothic skyscrapers, huge Gothic sky-scrapers covered with Gothic statues and things, monsters, lions, eagles—you know, Gothic shit. What do Gothic skyscrapers have to do with anything? you ask. It's to show you the character's psychology. Imagine you go to a party and they introduce you to somebody and he says 'How do you do? I make Gothic skyscrapers,' you'd be all like this, right? You'd be curious about the character's *psychology*."

Frank nods.

Chaz looks on in disgust.

"Exactly, you're all like this, because you're wondering, *What sort of psychology are we dealing with with this motherfucker?* And that's the reaction I want to provoke in the audience. To do that, I film all these construction sites with all these Gothic statues around, and the guy walking at night, walking among the statues . . ."

Frank makes a gesture with his hand, like, *Get on with it.*

"Right. Now, because he needs statues for his skyscrapers, he's got this smuggling thing going on with ancient statues, Egyptian, Persian, Indian, Oriental, whatever the fuck. Cut to one of these illegal yards, where they're wrapping up statues, talking Indian, some exotic fucking language. Right now he's got to go to Cairo to negotiate for a new consignment of these archaeological finds. But the FBI's got him under surveillance."

"Fucking bacons!" Frank says, and turns to Chaz with a smile, like he's trying to interest him in the story.

Chaz looks on in disgust.

"They got him under surveillance because . . . because . . . I still gotta figure that one out."

"They always find a reason," Chaz says, just to please Frank.

"There you go. Anyway, he's gotta go to Cairo and he doesn't want to make the FBI suspicious. So what does he do? you ask."

"What does he do?" Chaz asks, again to please Frank.

"He starts going after a pop star. He's very rich, lots of dough, he gets invited to a party, and there's this famous pop star there.

J-Lo. Let's call her J-Lo . . . He sees this fantastic ass and he goes after her. He's got the Egyptian looks, the dark clothes, the Arab mustache, he's catnip for the pop stars. He wears those really soft moccasins the pop stars like. So he invites her to his penthouse apartment for dinner, on the top floor of a Gothic skyscraper. And of course she goes . . . Spicy food . . . full of all that Oriental crap . . . bedroom worthy of a young fucking Omar Sharif . . . Except that once they're in the bedroom he starts to slap her around. At first J-Lo—she takes offense. Then she falls madly in love with him . . ."

"What a whore!" Chaz says, starting to enjoy this.

"Obviously, after he makes her fall in love with him, Omar refuses to take her calls. J-Lo cries and cries and the secretaries just keep slamming down the phone. Then, after letting her stew for a week, *he* calls *her*. At first she doesn't even answer, she's sure it's one of those trainers who are always trying to cheer her up, one of those guys who make you do bends to dispel the love toxins, crap like that. But the phone keeps ringing and she can't stand it anymore, so finally she answers, and it's him, inviting her to dinner in the most fashionable restaurant in New York.

"So . . . soft lights, Italian wine, duck *à l'orange*, candles, deluxe flatware, and Omar laughing, sitting on top of the world. J-Lo thinks he's happy because of her, but in fact he's laughing because a couple of hours earlier he called *Vanity Fair* and all the other fucking magazines and told them where to catch Jennifer Lopez with her new boyfriend. Omar goes on about Cairo, the casbah, and J-Lo's looking at him spellbound, her eyes full of passion and love, 'When will you take me there?' she asks him, and he says, 'I'll take you there soon, right now I have a lot of things to do here in New York and I can't just let them slide,' and he gives her a ring. Jennifer starts crying with joy, she's standing up to hug him . . . (imagine . . . the close-up of J-Lo's ass) when this tide of photographers and flashes descends on their table. Instinctively, she loses her temper, but then she sees him, with that mustache, and a sly smile, and she doesn't get it, J-Lo doesn't get it. He whispers, 'You can't keep love a secret,' or some such crap, and then Jennifer takes off her shoes, jumps on the table, and says to the photographers, 'I asked him if he's taking me to Cairo and he said yes, even though he's got a lot of things to do here in New York and can't just let them slide, isn't he a sweetheart?'"

"Shit! Apart from being a whore, she's a real bitch!" Chaz says.

"Shut up, Chaz," Frank says. "I like this concept, I like it a lot . . ."

SCALI'S AMARETTI

SCALI'S AMARETTI: the brass sign stands out against the volcanic stone of the building on Corso Italia, a small twenties building, with a stone base and a full complement of pediments and capitals and masks. Inside, an oak parquet floor, and mahogany counters with the amaretti beautifully displayed in pyramids on large silver platters.

Behind the counter opposite the entrance, Signorina Niscemi (the forty-seven-year-old sister of Cosimo Niscemi, Uncle Sal's childhood friend who died of a heart attack a while ago, leaving his sister Vittoria on her own, until she was charitably taken on by Uncle Sal as salesclerk, secretary, manageress, administrator, and figurehead of Scali's Amaretti) sticks out her chest and fixes herself up because she's just seen Uncle Sal open the front door, which is made of glass and brass.

Uncle Sal strides in, making the parquet floor creak.

"Are they here?" he says.

"No, *commendatore*," Signorina Nescimi says, "but they're definitely coming."

Uncle Sal looks worried. He walks to the counter on the left, then climbs the mahogany staircase that leads to the second floor. At the top, he stops in front of the first door on the left, opens it, and goes in.

Like a sergeant's flashlight, the light from the corridor reveals a couple of cans of beer on the floor. Uncle Sal goes quickly to the window and opens it wide. The room stinks of alcohol and smoke, and he can't help covering his mouth with his handkerchief. The desk is a mess: on the right, six partly eaten amaretti lined up in a row; on the left, a heap of beer cans, more amaretti, and empty gin bottles. Uncle Sal grabs the wastepaper basket and throws in the amaretti, bottles, and cans.

"The room's a mess," he hears someone say behind his back, while he's still bending over the basket. He stands up and sees Lou Sciortino in the doorway. *Minchia, the way he dresses!* Uncle Sal thinks, and for a moment he sees his own youth . . . Abby Lane, Xavier Cugat with that little dog of his, a dog for a faggot, Marino Barreto with his yellow shirt and shiny gray suits, just like the one Lou's wearing right now.

"It's a little . . . bit of a mess, I'm sorry, Don Scali . . ." Lou says.

"*Minchia*," Uncle Sal says, "I'm not surprised you got food poisoning!"

Lou looks around in silence. He knows Uncle Sal would like him to say, *Thank you, Don Scali, for taking me to the hospital*, but he doesn't want to give him the satisfaction.

"You sure gave us a fright," Uncle Sal says. "First you go all white, and then you faint in public."

Lou takes off his jacket, rolls up the sleeves of his yellow shirt to the elbow, walks to his chair, sits down, and puts his feet up on the desk.

Uncle Sal looks at the black patent-leather shoes planted there in front of his eyes. Then he pulls up his pants in order not to ruin their immaculate crease, and sits down on one of the two chairs in front of the desk. He crosses his hands on his stomach and rocks a little, then says, "This chair ain't all that solid, Lou, better not rock."

Lou opens a drawer in the desk and takes out a bottle of gin. "A drink?" he says.

"A drop, Lou, just a drop . . ." Uncle Sal says, looking at the glass with a disgusted expression. "You know the respect I got for your grandfather. It's a point of honor with me that you feel fine here, Lou!"

"I'm fine, Don Scali, don't worry."

"Good!" Uncle Sal says. "Good!" Then he looks around. "But now there are some new eventualities . . ."

Lou makes a face, like he's saying, *Eventualities, what the fuck is that?*

"I mean, something's happened . . ." Uncle Sal says, stroking the crease in his pants. "While you were unconscious in the hospital, it was like fucking Afghanistan here, flashing lights, sirens, TV news . . . What the fuck's going on? I asked Tuccio. Tuccio goes off to find out and when he comes back he's looking really grim like he's been to a funeral. You know what happened? A robbery at Uncle Mimmo's! They killed a sergeant!"

"Shit," Lou says.

"It's worse than if somebody had slashed my face," Uncle Sal says, "much worse! Because I know the boys in this neighborhood, every single one of them, and I know for sure that if they do a robbery they don't kill me any cops. So I asked around, made inquiries, and found out that right after the robbery some half-drugged bozo came out of Uncle Mimmo's store covered in blood."

Lou sips his gin and says nothing.

"If it was down to me," Uncle Sal says, "*first* I'd kill the son of a bitch with my own hands, *then* I'd ask him if it was him. But I gotta handle things differently here. Because you know who this junkie is? It's that guitarist who lives next door to Tony: Nick Palumbo!

Capito? The one Tony's so crazy about. He treats him like one of the family! Sure, you think about it, you know sometimes it happens, a good kid goes off the rails. Like they give you a couple fixes in San Berillo, and you become an addict and then they don't give you a fucking thing. So whaddaya do? To get another fix, you go do a robbery and kill some asshole with a badge.

"Anyway, Lou, sometimes a man can't just do what he oughta do. Sometimes it's better to use your head. Right now I gotta straighten things out here, I can't just let it end badly. And there's something else I gotta tell you, Lou! I need to fix things up for Mindy! Which is why I say: Are we sure it was him? Tell me, are you sure? No, you can't be, Lou! Which is why I gotta tell you this, too. I saw this Nick at my nephew's barbecue at the time of the robbery. *Minchia*, everybody there saw him talking to Mindy. So then I ask myself: If Nick Palumbo was at my nephew's barbecue at the time of the robbery, what was he doing at Uncle Mimmo's store?"

"What was he doing, Don Scali?" Lou asks.

"He wasn't doing nothing! Nothing whatsoever! The son of a bitch wasn't there! Have I made myself clear?"

"Totally, Don Scali."

"Good. And now we gotta make it clear to Uncle Mimmo, too," Uncle Sal says.

"Excuse me, Don Scali," Lou says, refilling his glass to the brim. "I don't want to be impolite, but I don't understand . . . What do you mean, 'We gotta make it clear'?"

"Lou, Lou, I'm under pressure right now to straighten things out . . . This is a very delicate matter. I can't send one of my *picciotti* to see Uncle Mimmo. I got my connections at police headquarters, but so does that son of a bitch Sonnino. Uncle Mimmo's an innocent. Let's say the police or Sonnino put the scare into him and he squeals that one of my *picciotti* threatened him . . . I gotta cover my back then . . . That's why you gotta do me a favor and go see Uncle

Mimmo, he won't know it was me who sent you, and that way we're okay, because even if he squeals he don't got nothing to squeal about."

Lou takes his feet off the desk, stands up, and paces the room, hands shoved in his pockets.

"Don Scali," he says, turning suddenly, "I'm honored that you thought of me for a delicate matter like this . . ."

"I gotta tell your grandfather you're a real good kid. I mean it . . . a good kid, real respectful. But the thing I don't want," Uncle Sal says, "the thing I don't want is this Nick, who's got a guilty conscience—though I don't understand why he's got a guilty conscience, seeing as how he was at the barbecue with us—deciding to take a powder. *Minchia*, he's a junkie, and junkies are nervous people, they scare easy. Let's say the bum takes off, how would I look with the police? He takes off, and everybody ends up thinking it really was him, and then the police get wise, and they come to me and say, '*Minchia*, Don Scali, your nephew's next-door neighbor kills a sergeant and, cock of the walk that you are, you don't know nothing about it? You don't know how to keep your own house in order?' In other words, Lou, it's all about keeping the dogs on the leash! Which is why it will help me if you keep an eye on this Nick, at least until we've made ourselves clear and persuaded him there's no reason to take off."

"My grandfather used to say that, too," Lou says.

"Keep the dogs on the leash?" Uncle Sal says. "My uncle used to say it . . . when he was loading his gun."

"No . . . cock of the walk . . ." Lou says. "Don Scali, how do I get to know this Nick?"

"Tony's throwing an engagement barbecue," Uncle Sal says, "a barbecue everybody in the neighborhood will remember all their lives. Nick Palumbo's invited, since he's the one getting engaged. You're invited, too. Tony's managed to get hold of some quail! Don't worry, there'll be plenty of gin!"

JASMINE JUST SPENT
HALF AN HOUR IN THE RED ROOM

Jasmine just spent half an hour in the red room of that pig Mr. Lewine's Politics & Prose Bookstore, and has no desire to hear any of Frank's bullshit.

"Jasmine," Frank Erra's saying, "when you read, you look just like Meadow Soprano. Whaddaya think, Chaz, is she or isn't she just like Tony and Carmela's daughter?"

"Meadow Soprano, the spitting image," Chaz says.

Jasmine doesn't bat an eyelid and carries on reading this fucking book, *Sicily: Complete Guide to the Island*, which had brought her into direct contact with that fat, circumcised bastard Lewine. When she asked him for a comprehensive guide to Sicily, the pig (the kind with a massive bald spot on top and long hair behind the ears, like two fucking brooms) pulled out half a dozen books: *Midnight in Sicily*, *Ciao Sicily*, *Sweet Sicily*, *In Sicily*, and other, similar crap. Then he told her there were others in the rare book section, known as the red room, ten feet by six and a half feet of paper and dust, rusty shelves, and a beat-up old desk. Lewine took out the books and handed them to her from behind, brushing against her, giving her what her mother, Ann Guardascione, used to call *'nu passaggio*. But Jasmine did leave with two books under her arm: *Ciao Sicily* by Damian Mandola, a book that mentions pasta with squash, fava beans, olives, and capers—Ann would have loved it—and this *Complete Guide* she's reading now to Frank.

"'This square owes its baroque harmony to the buildings that surround it. In the middle, the fountain of the Elephant, symbol of the city, a contrast to the more discreet nineteenth-century Amenano fountain on the south side, set against the del Chierici and Pardo palaces . . .'"

"Jasmine," Frank says, "you're not a college girl like Meadow! *Cazzarola!* Who gives a fuck about Sicilian baroque? Get on with it."

Jasmine angrily licks the middle finger of her right hand, leafs through about twenty pages, and stops at random. Then she starts reading again. "'One of its most famous citizens was Giovanni Verga, whose literary output, after his early commitment to patriotic themes, developed a predominantly sentimental and romantic vein . . .'"

Sentimental and romantic? A light goes on in Frank's mind.

"'In 1871,'" Jasmine continues, "'with the publication in Milan of *A Sparrow's Tale*, he achieved almost immediate success. The novel was first published in installments in the newspaper *La Ricamatrice* in 1870 . . .'"

La Ricamatrice! A Sparrow's Tale! Frank feels faint with happiness.

"Chaz," he says, "you remember that Zeffirelli movie *Sparrow*?"

"Who's Zeffirelli, Frank?" Chaz says. "A friend of Trent's?"

"Yes, you could say that," Frank says, very pleased with himself. "You could say that."

Just one hour later, Greta is still going *hmmm* in her mind. Frank's request was really strange. To say she isn't startled—yes, startled is the word—would be a lie. Frank's never sounded so nice on the phone. And not just on the phone. The fact is, Frank isn't what you'd call a nice person. Who could possibly call him nice? He always looks so unhappy. Even his ma couldn't call him nice, that's for sure! But who knows what Frank's ma is like, maybe she looks unhappy all the time, too! Anyway, what's clear is that Greta is going to Italy. My God, for the premiere of a Leonard Trent movie! Hmmm . . . Anyway, Frank was really strange. It's obvious he wants something from her. And not just the usual blow job, Frank's never gotten a blow job by being nice. So what does he want? Hmmm. The fear is always there, the fear that somebody like Frank will suddenly decide he needs to get his act together. It's something that comes to all men: they reach a certain age and they want to get married. *To somebody else* . . . Of course! Frank has fallen in love with some Carmela with a face like a lobster gone bad, and he wants to make her jealous by taking Greta to Italy. That's gotta be it. A man like Frank doesn't pull out the sweet talk unless he's got a guilty conscience. It's as plain as the nose on your face.

LOU IS ON VIA PACINI

Lou is on Via Pacini, a market street like a hundred others: the red varnished wooden pagoda of a Chinese restaurant, a greengrocer, a fish vendor, a bar, a butcher, an elegant perfume shop, a shop selling jackknives. Uncle Mimmo's store, though, is nowhere to be seen.

Lou glances again at the photo Uncle Sal gave him.

Tony, the hairdresser, is gazing at the guy called Nick with a sweet expression, too sweet for Lou, the same way that clotheshorse John Giuffré, the disgrace of the Giuffrés, looked at him at the last party Lou went to in New York.

Nick, on the other hand, looks like a bad copy of Tony. He's got an excessively sweet expression. He's imitating him.

Lou puts the photo back in his pocket and walks to the knife shop.

When Tano wakes up, in the afternoon, he goes to see Uncle Mimmo in his store, since there are no customers at Uncle Mimmo's in the afternoon. That's because Uncle Mimmo only stocks the kind of thing no one would ever buy in the afternoon, except, obviously, in an emergency, like Band-Aids or rubbing alcohol. So Tano goes there, sits on the stepladder, and at dusk he shakes an item or two off the shelves. This is because, as darkness falls, Uncle Mimmo also falls, slowly collapsing on the counter. Since Tano is reluctant to wake a man in the middle of his nap and risk giving offense, he knocks the Dash to the floor. At which Uncle Mimmo jumps, gets up, and turns on the light.

And Tano nods.

The knife shop is as brightly lit as an autopsy room. Lou nods casually to the salesclerk and starts looking in the display cases. Lined up neatly on the glass shelves, with the handwritten price tags, are dozens of jackknives. None of those big jagged knives you find in America, twenty inches long and with a first-aid kit in the handle, or those sophisticated brass knuckles tailor-made for schizos in Texas or Arkansas or some psychopath in New York. The knives here are small, with carefully inlaid handles, and the brass knuckles are discreet, practical, functional.

"Can I help you?" Lou turns and sees that the salesclerk isn't a salesclerk. He smells very strongly of aftershave, a fiftyish man dressed to the nines like a wiseguy, and is clearly the owner. A scar runs across his face, fittingly enough, it occurs to Lou, in a shop like this.

Lou looks around him, then looks straight at Scarface and says, "You got any grafting knives?"

Every time he turns on the light, Uncle Mimmo screws up his eyes and listens out for the noise. Because every time he turns on the light, Uncle Mimmo hears a buzzing. He's never been able to figure out if it's a lightbulb buzzing, the flies waking up, or something else. As always, he looks questioningly at Tano, and Tano also screws up his eyes and listens carefully, and then, being the honest person he is, shakes his head. In response, Uncle Mimmo looks at him like he's the biggest deadbeat on the face of the earth. Then he turns back to the counter and picks up his magazine, no point in talking to somebody who refuses to hear the buzzing. It's always the *same* magazine: one of the first illustrated magazines with color printing and lots of photographs. Uncle Mimmo likes those photographs, why he should buy another one?

Scarface is smiling slightly. "Follow me," he says, putting his hands in his pockets and making the contents jangle. He goes behind the counter, bends, and comes back up with a velvet-lined drawer. Inside, grafting knives so stylish they wouldn't look out of place in a jeweler's window.

"It's nice," he says as Lou examines the merchandise, "to see a young guy like you still interested in grafting knives. Most young guys today just want knives with points. Try telling them you don't need a point. I always say there's nothing you can do with a knife that's got a point that you can't do with a knife that don't got a point. You just gotta think about it to see it's true: you don't need a point."

Lou, with a knife in his hand, looks up questioningly.

"I mean, let's say you're hunting. What fucking use is a knife that's got a point? You want to kill a rabbit, you use a rifle, right? The only thing you need a knife for is to skin it, and if you skin a rabbit with a knife that's got a point you're gonna prick yourself, right? You may say, 'A knife that's got a point can be useful for finishing the rabbit off,' but that's where you'd be wrong! When did you ever see anyone with any *intelligence* kill a rabbit with a knife? Those rabbits can really bite, you know. So let's say you don't kill the rabbit and it turns around and bites you. Rabbit bites are dangerous . . . No, you want to kill a rabbit, you take a rifle and blow its brains out. Knives are for other things. For those things you don't need a point."

Lou looks at him. "I understand," he says, and goes back to examining the knives.

Scarface gives a flashy smile, like he's saying, *Of course you understand.* Then he goes on, "But young guys today, they don't know these things, there's nobody to explain it to them. They go hunting and they fuck up big-time. There used to be people who could explain things to you," he says, rubbing his cheek.

"I'll take this, don't bother wrapping it up for me."

It's a knife with a mother-of-pearl handle as white and shiny as his grandfather's hair.

"Listen," Lou says as he pays, "I could use some shaving foam, you know anywhere around here I can buy some?"

"Sure! Next door, at Uncle Mimmo's. The entrance is just a hole in the wall and there's no sign, but you'll find shaving foam there, he's got every brand!"

When Lou steps out onto the street again, there's a weak yellow light coming out of Uncle Mimmo's general store. The entrance is a small wood and glass door wedged in between the knife shop and the perfume shop.

Lou enters, resolute.

Mimmo hasn't got time to say, "Please wait outside and I'll . . ." Lou is already inside, standing in front of the counter with his hands in the pockets of his raincoat, looking straight at him.

"He must need Band-Aids, that's why he's in a hurry," a voice says behind him. Lou turns in surprise and sees Tano sitting on the stepladder, huddled against a metal shelf full of detergents.

"I told you to wait outside, can't you see there's people here?"

"No, it's okay, don't worry, I'm fine," Tano says politely.

"No, wait," Uncle Mimmo says, being a stickler for order in his store. "It's a matter of principle. If I say wait in line, I say it for a reason, right? So please, do me the courtesy of going outside, and then, when I tell you, you can come in. We finish our business calmly here, and then . . . then we attend to you."

Lou passes a hand over his face. Then he goes out.

The owner of the knife shop is standing in the doorway smoking a cigarette. When he sees Lou, he bows slightly in greeting and goes on smoking.

Lou blinks.

From Uncle Mimmo's general store there's a noise like a subway train passing. Then the sound of Uncle Mimmo shouting, "*Minchia*, I knew it!"

The owner of the knife shop opens his arms wide. Then he continues smoking.

Lou blinks and clenches his lower jaw.

Uncle Mimmo appears in the doorway and says, "Come in, I put Tano in the men's toiletries section."

The owner of the knife shop turns to Uncle Mimmo and bows in greeting.

Uncle Mimmo reciprocates. "You know, the section of the late lamented," he says with a resigned expression.

The owner of the knife shop opens his arms wide, like he's saying, *What can you do?*

Uncle Mimmo nods, like he's saying, *You're right.* Then he follows Lou into the store.

Tano pokes his head out of the men's toiletries section and says, "Good evening," to Lou, like he hasn't seen him before.

Uncle Mimmo silences him with a look. Tano starts looking casually at the aftershaves.

"So, what kind of Band-Aid do you need?" Uncle Mimmo asks, putting on his glasses.

Tano nods, looking at an aftershave.

Lou takes the grafting knife out of his pocket and puts it on the counter. Then he takes out the photo and places it next to the knife.

Uncle Mimmo looks at the knife. Then he looks at the photo, then at Lou. Then he takes out the crossbow.

Lou blinks. He passes a hand over his face.

Tano drops the aftershave.

"The Commander says that officially this is used to kill rats," Uncle Mimmo says. "But that's hard to believe, because to kill rats with this first you gotta corner them, and that's the hardest thing with rats."

"Do you know the guy in the photo?" Lou asks, pretending he hasn't seen the crossbow.

Uncle Mimmo looks at him. Then, without putting down the crossbow, he glances at the photo. "Sure, it's Tony, the hairdresser."

"Oh, yes, Tony, the hairdresser, I know him, too," Tano says.

Uncle Mimmo gives him a dirty look.

"Tony . . ." Tano says, and then doesn't know what else to say, so he looks around.

"Not him, the other one," Lou says.

Uncle Mimmo raises his eyebrows. He permits himself another glance. "No," he says, "I don't know that one. But who the fuck are you?"

"Good question," Lou says. "Let's just say I'm somebody who's here to give you a piece of advice."

"Let me see, maybe I know him . . ." Tano says.

"Shut up, you don't know him, either," Uncle Mimmo says.

Tano looks around.

"What . . . advice would that be?" Uncle Mimmo says.

"If anybody else asks you the same question, give the same answer. Do we understand each other?"

"Hmmm," Uncle Mimmo says, screwing up his eyes. "But what if I suddenly realize I *have* seen this guy?"

"You'd be wrong."

"Why?"

Lou thinks about it. Then he says, "Because at the time of the robbery this guy here was at Tony's barbecue, so you didn't see him."

"Oh, right," Uncle Mimmo says.

"Precisely," Lou says.

"Precisely," Tano says.

"Do we understand each other?" Lou says.

"Oh, yes, we understand each other," Uncle Mimmo says, putting away the crossbow. "But that's not the point."

"No?" Lou says.

"No," Uncle Mimmo says. Calmly, he sits down on the stool, folds his arms, and says, "Listen . . . how about we stop talking in code?"

Tano nods.

"In code?" Lou says.

"I mean, why don't we talk clearly?" Uncle Mimmo says.

"Okay, let's talk clearly."

"Right. First," Uncle Mimmo says, raising his thumb, "I don't understand the way you guys work these days. In the old days, we all understood and we got along fine. Now everything's fucked up. *Minchia*, first you don't want to ask for protection, then you rob me, and now you come and threaten me! Look at me, I got white hair! I'm a quiet guy who minds his own business. Besides, excuse me, but don't you still got your arrangement with the police? *Minchia*, you used to be better organized, and with all due respect you didn't used to fuck up quite so much. Don't you know that when the police guy wanted to do an Identi-Kit picture I made him draw a baking pan?"

"A baking pan?"

"Right, that's what I told him. From all I could see, with a shovelful of the sergeant's brains all over my face, the murderer was the spitting image of a baking pan. Apart from the fact that even if I did see him, do you people think I'd cough up the name of somebody who blows a sergeant's face off?"

Tano shakes his head, *Absolutely not.*

"Secondly." Uncle Mimmo raises his thumb again. And with the same thumb, he presses the button that opens the cash register, jumping at the TA-TANG as usual.

"Who the fuck makes these registers?" he says. "They give you a brain hemorrhage every time you wanna make change!" Then he sighs, calmly takes out a wad of banknotes, moistens his thumb and index finger with his tongue, and starts counting. One, two, three, four . . . fifteen.

"Here, here's a hundred and fifty euros. Taking into consideration goodwill, position, neighborhood, clientele, and any other fucking thing you want to consider, I think the price is right. Now just do me the pleasure of taking these euros and giving them to whoever sent you. Then next month on the dot, come back and I'll do what you want. And tell whoever sent you that Uncle Mimmo is perfectly happy to pay protection. As long as he's left alone. Do we understand each other?"

Tano coughs.

"So, do we understand each other?"

Tano coughs.

Uncle Mimmo looks at him.

"Cosimo . . ." Tano says.

"Oh, yes, *minchia*, right." He starts counting again, and puts down another fifteen ten-euro bills. "Same thing for the bar opposite, Cosimo, remember that, Co-si-mo. Next month you can go directly to him, I'll warn him in advance."

Lou looks at the money and nods. He takes the cash and the photo and the knife, and puts them all in his pocket.

"So, we done here or what?" Uncle Mimmo says.

Lou nods.

"Could you use a crossbow? I'll give it to you, I don't need it anymore."

Lou looks at him and says, "Thanks a lot, just wrap it up for me."

IN THE LOBBY OF THE HOTEL, DON GIORGINO IS SLURPING AN *ORZATA*

I n the lobby of the hotel, Don Giorgino is slurping an *orzata*.
From time to time he adjusts his round sunglasses. Every time
he takes a slurp he leans on his cane, and when he puts down
the glass his frail hand shakes. His two foot soldiers, his *picciotti*,
make sure he doesn't spill the *orzata*.

"Where's Vicienzo?" he asks.

The two *picciotti* look at each other. "Don Giorgino, we found
out Vicienzo was a rat, don't you remember?"

Don Giorgino Favarotta nods. "Are we taking care of his family?"

The two *picciotti* look at each other. Vicienzo was known as
Vicienzo Scannafamigghia, "Vicienzo Who Killed His Family,"
because at the age of thirteen he stabbed his father, mother, and
brother in the stomach. He never married and in later life was alone
in the world. "Of course, Don Giorgino, don't worry."

Don Giorgino nods, picks up the *orzata*, and slurps it. His hand
shakes as he puts down the glass.

The two *picciotti* lean forward, their eyes on the glass. It didn't
spill this time, either.

Don Giorgino leans with both his hands on the cane he's holding tight between his legs.

'Nzino parks in front of the Central Palace Hotel on Via Etnea, near the Bellini Gardens. It's a pedestrian zone, but Sal Scali's Mercedes is allowed to park there. He gets out, goes the long way around the car, and opens the door for Uncle Sal.

Uncle Sal gets out, buttons up his jacket, puts on his sunglasses, and walks into the hotel.

When you've got an appointment with a big shot, it's good manners to come alone, without your *picciotti*.

And Uncle Sal is indebted to Don Giorgino Favarotta.

It was Don Giorgino Favarotta, who was born in Trapani but moved to Catania when he was a child, who first suggested to Uncle Sal that he decapitate Alfio, and who subsequently supported him as a candidate when the Vaccalluzzos, whom Uncle Sal's predecessor Mimmo Asciolla answered to, demanded an explanation. Don Giorgino intervened and the Vaccalluzzos had to back off. The fact was, Don Giorgino liked Sal Scali. A few years back, in a youthful fit of anger, Don Giorgino had had Natale Impellizzeri from Marzamemi killed because of a supposed slight, without taking into account the Impellizzeris' connections with the Guarreras of Pozzallo, and the Guarreras' connections with the Gullottas of San Vito lo Capo. For this reason, Carmine Gullotta had sentenced Giorgino Favarotta to death.

And it was Sal Scali, still very young at the time, who straightened things out.

In Naples, Uncle Sal had met Ciro La Bruna, who was really a top-class greaseball, being related to the *americani*. Ciro La Bruna sent a message to Carmine Gullotta that the La Brunas had "done away with" Natale Impellizzeri because he was fucking with the Secondigliano Alliance. Carmine Gullotta made inquiries and sent a message to Ciro La Bruna informing him that Natale Impellizzeri didn't even know what the fuck the Secondigliano Alliance was. And Ciro La Bruna, being the top guy he was, sent a message to Carmine Gullotta saying, "Sorry, Don Carmine, we must have made a mistake."

Carmine Gullotta was left speechless.

In return, every now and again Don Giorgino Favarotta has to cut the La Brunas in on a job being done by some crew up in the north, and every now and again he and Sal Scali have to perform a service for the La Brunas of Forcella and America.

In the hotel bar, Uncle Sal spots the three men and walks toward them deferentially. The meeting is taking place in a hotel because that's what protocol requires. Don Giorgino has to reprimand Uncle Sal in public and tell him to straighten out this sergeant business. To do this, he can't invite Uncle Sal to his house, he can't threaten a guest who's paying a social call, *he* has to go to Sal. And he can't go to his house, because his family and kids are there.

"Don Giorgino," Uncle Sal says, "you're here."

And he stands there, waiting for a sign.

Don Giorgino doesn't move.

One of his *picciotti* goes up to Don Giorgino and whispers in his ear, "Sal Scali's here."

Don Giorgino jumps. "Turuzzeddu is here?"

"Here I am, Don Giorgino!"

"Here he is," the *picciotto* says.

"So why don't you tell him to sit down?" Don Giorgino says to the *picciotto*.

The *picciotto* signals to Uncle Sal that he can sit down.

Uncle Sal sits down and looks around him.

"Is it true Turuzzeddu fucked up?" Don Giorgino asks the *picciotto* on his right.

"It's true, Don Giorgino, I fucked up!" Uncle Sal says.

"It's true, he tells me," Don Giorgino says. Then he turns to the *picciotto* on his left. "Is it true or not that I always say, when somebody fucks up they gotta put it right?"

"It's true," the *picciotto* confirms.

"It's true!" Uncle Sal says.

Don Giorgino nods and turns to the *picciotto* on his right. "I know if Turuzzeddu fucks up, we gotta give him time to put it right. He's a quick thinker, I'm sure he'll straighten things out within a week, because I got some business to take care of in town next week, and I need everything to be clean. *Minchia*," he says, laughing his toothless laugh, "it's a good thing Turuzzeddu's a quick thinker, otherwise I'd be in the shit!"

The *picciotto* turns to Uncle Sal and says, "Don Giorgino is sure you'll straighten things out in a week."

"Tell Don Giorgino that Sal Scali has already straightened things out."

"Sal Scali says—"

"I heard him, what do you think I am, deaf?" Don Giorgino says. "Why don't you two boys go for a walk? Did you hear? Turuzzeddu's already straightened things out. Now sit here, and tell me about it." He squeezes the arm of the *picciotto* on the left and says, "Turuzzeddu says he's straightened things out, then he has. You think somebody's going to say things are straightened out when they're not?"

The *picciotti* look at each other, take off their dark glasses, and go out without a word.

Once they're alone, Uncle Sal sits down on the chair next to Don Giorgino.

"Turuzzeddu, tell me about it!" Don Giorgino says.

"Everything's fine," Uncle Sal says, "just like you ordered. Tonight, that kid Sciortino meets the junkie. He already went to see Uncle Mimmo and threatened him . . . That way, like you ordered, we talk to the cops, tell them the *americano* is trying to fuck things up for Sal Scali, shifting the blame from that junkie dipshit onto two of my *picciotti* who just happened to be passing through Uncle Mimmo's store! He's trying to make the cops think I'm some nobody whose word's for shit—that's our line. But he who lives by the sword . . ."

"Takes it in the ass!" Don Giorgino says. "Please, I need everything in place for next week, the La Brunas are sending us that package from America, and we gotta get it delivered."

LOU SCIORTINO SENIOR LIVED IN BROOKLYN UNTIL NOT SO LONG AGO

Lou Sciortino Senior lived in Brooklyn until not so long ago. Now he's got a beautiful house in New Jersey, horses by de Chirico on the walls, a grand piano in the living room, and *picciotti* in the garden, all spruced up. But Don Lou hasn't felt comfortable since he left Brooklyn. In Brooklyn, Catherine and Charles Scorsese were his neighbors, they were so proud of their boy. All his dreams are there, all his experiences. Fuck, Vincente Minnelli in person once knocked at his door. He was a bit too scented for Don Lou's taste, Don Lou was just a boy then, an ambitious boy, but he already knew how to spot a limp wrist. He went with him to a party, Gambino's orders, to make sure nobody insulted him. Fuck, what a party! Everybody was there! Marilyn, Joe, but above all the man himself, Frank, you just had to look at him to know he had three balls! Lou Sciortino Senior later told everybody what had happened. How he asked Frank Sinatra for a cigarette, and Frank said, "Sorry, kid, I haven't got one," and he said, "Don't matter, Frank," and Frank said, "Hey, kid, what's your name?" and he said, "Lou Sciortino," and Frank said, "Wait there, Lou," and went out and came back with a huge silver tray full of cigarettes. Don Lou subsequently read the same story in a magazine, told by some fucking actor, and his first reaction was that the fucking actor was a son of a bitch who'd ripped off his story, but then he thought maybe the real son of a bitch was Frank, who must have scripted the entire scene.

But what Don Lou remembers most of all from Brooklyn and his youth is Saul Trento. Lou and Saul, everybody said in Brooklyn. Saul Trento was more than a friend, he was his brother, even though he wasn't Sicilian, but was born in Bacoli, a little village near Naples. At a certain point, all the Trentos decided to move to Pennsylvania. Don Lou said to Saul, "What the fuck you going there for? There's nothing there but cowboys!" Saul lasted only a couple of months in Pennsylvania, then came back to Brooklyn, worked a couple of jobs with Lou, and married Jenny Tagliacozzo. It wasn't until the wedding, a nice Jewish wedding with all the usual complaining, that Lou even realized Saul was Jewish. *Minchia*, a Jew from Bacoli, near Naples! But Saul really loved Lou. He loved him so much that when he died very young, Lou secretly helped Jenny, and then Jenny's children and Jenny's children's children, including Leonard, the degenerate grandson who'd seen fit to take the "o" off his name.

When Don Lou got the idea to launder a little money by making movies, he naturally thought of Leonard, who wanted to be like Catherine and Charles's boy. The kid pissed him off at first, thought he was an artist after some idiot at *The Village Voice* called him one. Then he understood: movies and construction, brilliant!

"So, Leonard, how's your old maid cousin in Pennsylvania?" Don Lou is sipping Amaretto Di Saronno, with two ice cubes, in the living room of his beautiful house in New Jersey. Leonard Trent has come to tell him about all the things that have been happening at Starship, the conversation with Erra, the premiere in Italy, shit like that.

"She's getting married next week, Don Lou!" Leonard says. "She met a widowed dentist in a fucking half-empty movie theater in Pennsylvania, during a showing of *Tenors*."

"*Minchia*, sometimes we do good deeds!" Don Lou says.

"Many times, Don Lou, many times! I can't imagine Starship in the hands of a suckass like Frank Erra!"

"What kind of guy is he?"

"Five feet something of overdressed lard, Don Lou."

"I mean, how is he . . . as a person? Conceited . . . modest?"

"In Neapolitan, my father would have said he's a *meza cazetta*, a nobody, Don Lou!"

"He's a buffer, Leonard! All buffers are *meza cazettas*! You can't put somebody with too much brains between you and the *picciotti*, because somebody with too much brains, sooner or later he's going to put you between the *picciotti* and him . . . John La Bruna's nobody's fool. He picked the right guy for the job!"

"What should I do, Don Lou?" Leonard asks timidly. "Should I go to Italy?"

"Mmmm . . ." Don Lou says, placing his glass on the little table next to the armchair. "Frank Erra doesn't give orders, he carries them out . . . The only reason he wants to go to Italy is because John La Bruna's told him to go to Italy . . . Because . . . because . . ."

Leonard Trent waits respectfully, saying nothing. Don Lou presses down on the armrests of his chair with his hands and gets to his feet with a groan.

"Because . . . You know what? I'm going to call my grandson in Catania right now. We're going to Italy together!" he says. "While I still got some juice in me . . . I'd like to see Rome and Catania one last time."

Faced with that old man, that white hair, those bright blue eyes staring right into his, and that incredibly straight back, Leonard finds it hard to contain his emotions. *Fuck!* he thinks. *That's how my grandpa must have been: tall, upright, with that look that sends shivers down your spine! Men with balls, damn it, not backslappers like us!*

Leonard doesn't know his grandfather was short, with a slightly curved spine and a gentle face, because Jenny Tagliacozzo lost all the photographs of her beloved Saul in a fire.

NUNZIO AND AGATINO
ARE DEEP IN THOUGHT

unzio and Agatino are deep in thought. They're wearing their dress uniforms, which they always wear when there's an important customer like Signora Zappulla in Tony's salon. Tony had them made to exactly match the uniforms in a seventies sci-fi series, the main characters of which did in fact look like hairdressers.

Tony's salon, on Via Umberto, is a cross between a seventies nightclub and an eighties Brazilian disco. The reason is that Uncle Sal, although he doesn't play an active part in the business, thought he could take advantage of the opportunity to launder some cash. This is the way it goes: You buy all the building and decorating materials in one of those warehouses in northern Italy where you can find anything, from a leopardskin couch to a glitter ball, and pay with a postdated check. Then you resell everything to yourself or some figurehead at a markup. The more you buy, the more you launder. That's why glitter balls are so expensive in Catania. "Tony, you want a marble floor?"

"Uncle, what can I say? . . . Every saint needs his chapel! That'd be fantastic!"

"Write it down, Tuccio, marble floor. Tony, you want Doric columns?" Tony's eyes shone. "Write it down, Tuccio, Doric columns."

Nunzio and Agatino also have the same muttonchop mustaches as the characters in that seventies series. Agatino, who lifts weights and is, as Signora Zappulla says, pointlessly tall, is wearing Japanese flip-flops that reveal little wisps of yellow hair on his big toes. Nunzio, on the other hand, who is short, is wearing platform shoes six inches high.

They're deep in thought because Signora Zappulla has already been shampooed, and needs her hair done for the political dinner tonight, and Tony hasn't yet appeared.

"You don't suppose he had problems with the paper, do you?" Signora Zappulla says anxiously. She's a well-preserved woman about fifty, a beautiful woman, except for her voice.

"Who, Tony?" Agatino says vaguely, trying to peer out the door.

"You know, Signora Falsaperla, Tony's giving Signora Zappulla the house special today," Nunzio says, getting ready to shampoo Signora Falsaperla.

"Do me a favor!" Signora Falsapera says, lying stretched out like a woman in labor, with her legs in the air and her feet nude because Nunzio has just finished giving her a pedicure. To help the polish dry, he's put cotton between her toes, which are as swollen as giant slugs.

The house special at Tony's is pieces of colored paper inserted in the hairdo to match the customer's clothes. Tony has also tried inserting Caltagirone ceramics, little pieces of volcanic rock, sea stones from Letojanni, and terra-cotta tiles, but the customers prefer colored paper.

"There's a political dinner at my house tonight," Signora Zappulla says, "and Tony is giving me paper inserts in the colors of my husband's coalition."

"I always tell Tano he should go into politics," Signora Falsaperla says. "If you can run a butcher's shop, you can run a country. Not like the guests on Bruno Vespa's talk show, who don't even know the price of a kilo of beef. Ask my husband Tano, he'll tell you how much it is! Actually, in our shop it's a bit more because we only sell beef from Argentina . . ."

"In my opinion, politics is too serious, you need to lighten things up a bit," Signora Zappulla says. "Have you noticed that on Vespa's show, when those bimbos from the gossip columns are on, they always talk about cooking? *Minchia*, here, before we sit down to eat we have to give our condolences for the people in the coalition who got killed!"

"Why?" Signora Falsaperla says. "Did they just kill some people in your husband's coalition?"

"Don't you read the newspapers?" Signora Zappulla says.

"Of course I read them," Signora Falsaperla says resentfully, "but I don't pay them any attention!"

"Three days ago, they killed the head of the cultural commission in Baulì!" Signora Zappulla says.

"Oh, that was because he was screwing somebody's wife . . . Heads of cultural commissions never have any money," Signora Falsaperla says.

"Well, I don't know about that," Signora Zappulla says, going back to leafing through a newspaper. "Anyway, I'm having my hair colored, to lighten things up. By the way, is Tony coming, or did they kill him, too?"

Nunzio and Agatino exchange a glance.

Tony has forgotten to get out of the car.

He's parked not far from the salon in his purple Fiat 127. He's also wearing a dress uniform, he has his hands on the steering wheel, which is covered in blue plush, and he's staring into space. A scented rubber flying saucer hangs from the rearview mirror, still swaying.

He's listening to "Tragedy" by the Bee Gees.

'Nzino is a mute. That is, he can hear and all his vocal equipment is in the right place, but he's never spoken a word in his life. His mother had the same psychological defect, that was why his father married her. And that's also why Uncle Sal hired 'Nzino as a driver.

So, today, when Uncle Sal said, "Why the fuck are you stopping again? Tony's salon, I said! I knew you were mute, but deaf, no!" 'Nzino couldn't say, "Look, you didn't say a fucking thing!" He started the car and set off. It was a bumpy ride, because whenever they go to Tony's salon, 'Nzino gets a little nervous. If he wasn't wearing gloves his hands would be sweaty.

Aunt Carmela's white hair appears at the door to Tony's salon.

Agatino and Nunzio look at each other. "*Mioddio!*" Agatino says in a low voice, because he's worked in Milan. "*E bona notte e sunatura!*" Nunzio murmurs, never having been outside Catania—Sicilian for, "We're fucked."

"*Buongiorno*, signora!" Agatino says heroically. "What a pleasant surprise. Don't tell me . . . don't tell me . . . we're finally getting rid of all that ugly white!"

Aunt Carmela looks at Agatino like he doesn't exist, walks with her chest out and her head high to a kind of Victorian throne, sits down, hugs her handbag to her chest, and says, "Firstly, I'm not signora, I'm signorina. Secondly, I'm not here for a hairdo. Thirdly, I came because I've got an appointment with my nephew, where is he?"

"I'm waiting for him, too," Signora Zappulla says. "I've got a political dinner tonight and Tony's not here."

"Dear Signora Zappulla," Aunt Carmela says, "I didn't recognize you with that cloth on your silly little head!"

Nunzio and Agatino exchange a glance.

Tragedy . . .

The tape finishes. Tony is about to rewind it, then suddenly comes to his senses. "*Minchia,*" he says. He gets out of the car, locks the door, and runs across the busy Via Umberto, ass wobbling.

He walks into the salon, all calm and collected, like he's just come back from having a drink at a bar.

"Hello, everybody. Signora Zappulla, my respects." Tony bows and kisses her hand. "Signora Falsaperla, my compliments." He walks in Signora Falsaperla's direction, but the sight of her lying there like a woman in labor, letting her nail polish dry, is too much even for him, so he does a half pirouette and finds himself face to face with Aunt Carmela.

"*Zia,* you're here."

"Yes, I'm here."

Tony kisses her on the cheek and says in her ear, "*Minchia, Zia,* it's lucky you came. You know Uncle Sal is plotting something, as usual. Let me tell you about it."

"What the hell have you been doing, Tony? I've been waiting half an hour," Signora Zappulla says.

"Nunzio, get the paper and we'll do Madame Zappulla," Tony says.

Nunzio turns off the water he's been using to shampoo Signora Falsaperla and goes into the back room.

"Tony," Signora Falsaperla says, with her head still in the washstand, "I want you to give me the house special next week, too, I'm going to the prefect's dinner. We gave him a good deal on the meat. *The prefect!*"

Tony looks at Agatino, like he's saying, *Will those two never leave each other the fuck alone?*

Avoiding Tony's gaze, Agatino folds the towel he's been using to massage Signora Zapulla's scalp.

"But of course, Madame Falsaperla!" Tony says.

"In my opinion, that prefect hasn't got long to live, the little shit," Signora Zappulla says under her breath.

"Okay, this is fine. Park here, 'Nzino. Go in and ask my nephew to come out. I'm not going into a place where they take it up the ass," Uncle Sal says.

'Nzino blinks nervously. He double-parks, switches off the engine, gets out of the car, and walks to the sidewalk.

Nunzio returns from the back room carrying the rolls of colored paper. Tony snatches them out of his hands. "Here," he says, "Madame Zappulla, these are all for you . . ."

'Nzino comes in. He looks around nervously. He spots Tony, and makes the usual sign with his thumb. Tony looks at Aunt Carmela. Aunt Carmela nods.

"But . . . but . . . but . . ." Tony says, "but . . . you didn't do the treatment!"

Agatino looks at him. *Treatment, what fucking treatment?*

Tony takes the rolls of paper, throws them angrily on the floor, and grinds them with the heel of his shoe.

"You're crazy! Completely crazy! You ought to be working in a bakery, or a butcher sh—I mean a bar! Signora Zappulla comes in here and you don't give her the treatment. Are you morons or what?

I tell you what I'm going to do, I'm going to step outside, walk to the newsstand, buy a copy of *Vanity Fair* to calm myself down, and when I come back I want to see Signora Zappulla having her treatment! Signora . . . signora . . . you tell me what you want me to do. If you tell me to fire them, I'll fire them!"

Tony looks at Nunzio and Agatino and winks at them, then grabs 'Nzino by the arm and rushes outside.

"What is this treatment?" Signora Zappulla asks Agatino suspiciously.

"To tell the truth, signora, it slipped my mind. Please forgive me, I was up late last night, there was a new club opening, wasn't there, Nunzio?"

"A really nice club—it's the hot new place."

"Nunzio, pass me the treatment and I'll do it right now!"

"What is this treatment?" Signora Falsaperla asks, taking her head out of the washstand and sitting up.

"Something special, signora."

"In that case, I want it, too."

"Of course, signora, of course."

'Nzino walks Tony to the car like he's supporting a child who's fainted. Tony takes one step and sways, takes another and feels dizzy. When they get to the car, 'Nzino opens the door for him.

"Thanks, thanks," Tony says, sitting down next to Uncle Sal.

Uncle Sal looks at him for a moment, then turns and looks out the window. "I was just passing by," he says.

The day Tony hired Nunzio and Agatino, Uncle Sal stopped by and told him about a transvestite who'd joined the hookers in San Berillo, "and you wouldn't believe the line of cars! Anyway, they gave him the operation for free, did you read in the papers?"

Tony started sweating. "But Uncle, why are you telling me these things?"

"Just making conversation," Uncle Sal said. "By the way, those new boys, have they got girlfriends?"

Tony's blood sugar level dropped precipitately. Uncle Sal was innocently asking questions, according to him, because an American friend of his had said apprentices should have girlfriends or wives because that way they were more attached to their work. But Tony didn't know that at the time. "NO!" he cried out. "They haven't got girlfriends!"

"You did the right thing, stopping by," Tony says now.

Uncle Sal nods. Of course he did the right thing. "Listen, you remember Nick?"

Tony doesn't answer.

Uncle Sal continues looking out the window. "I been thinking about him."

"Oh," Tony says.

"I wanna forgive him."

"Oh."

"And you know why?"

Tony shakes his head.

"Because," Uncle Sal says, turning to look at him, "he made the whole family look like shit. Not just me, not just you. Oh, no! He really made the whole family look like shit. Like he was doing it on purpose. Because where do you find the whole Scali family together? At Tony's barbecue. And that deadbeat made the whole family look bad in front of the guests!"

"But . . . Uncle . . . look . . ."

"Shut up," Uncle Sal says. "Now, I've either gotta forgive him or kill him. Which do you prefer, Tony . . . ?"

Tony looks at him, stunned, and says nothing.

"No point in asking the question, huh, Tony?" Uncle Sal says. "Because you like the deadbeat . . . In fact, I'm sure you'd like it if he became part of the family, right? Correct me if I'm wrong."

Tony says nothing. He's got a look on his face like somebody who's turned in on himself, somebody who's repeating obsessively, *My sugar level's dropping, please leave me alone.*

"Fuck, Tony," Uncle Sal says, "don't piss me off. I told you to correct me if I'm wrong. Maybe you think I'm wrong?"

"No, Uncle Sal . . . it's just my sugar level's dropping and—"

"Who gives a shit about your sugar level, Tony?" Uncle Sal says. "Stop busting my balls!"

"As a matter of fact, Uncle Sal," Tony says, "I do like Nick and I'd be happy if—"

"Good, Tony, good! *Minchia*, you've convinced me! Throw a nice barbecue tomorrow night, and we'll see if Nick and Mindy are making eyes at each other."

"So I invite . . . just Nick and Mindy?" Tony says.

"Tony! Tony! It's not your sugar that's dropping, it's your brain! You gotta invite EVERYBODY! EVERYBODY! *Minchia*, what do I gotta do to make my nephews and nieces happy?" Uncle Sal says.

At Tony's, Agatino is scientifically demonstrating the principle that flattery is best used, not for the sake of ingratiation, but for distracting the other person while you shovel shit under the rug. It's the explanation for a lot of things, you know. Why, for example, do you think Uncle Sal behaves that way? Anyway . . . Applying distilled water like it was some kind of miracle potion, Agatino says, "Signorina Carmela is a woman of the old school, isn't that right, signorina? She likes to keep her hair white, because it's a sign of wisdom, isn't that right, signorina? Anyway . . . I say it's nice that in Sicily you can find people with such different lives existing side by side. Isn't that right, Nunzio?"

Nunzio nods fervently.

"A woman like Signorina Carmela so . . . proudly rooted in tradition, that's what they say, isn't it, Signora Zappulla? And someone like you, oriented toward the future, emancipated, dynamic . . ." Agatino has run out of adjectives.

". . . open to innovation, part of the social fabric, motivated by a sense of equal opportunity!" Nunzio says, blushing.

"She's a woman, let's don't forget," Agatino says, "like you, Signora Falsaperla, a woman . . . a woman . . ."

Signora Falsaperla lifts her head from the washstand, her curiosity aroused.

"Here he is . . ." Agatino looks at Nunzio. Nunzio looks at Agatino.

Tony comes in, shaking, white-faced, sweating, out of breath, with *Vanity Fair* under his arm. "Are you doing the treatment?"

"Sure, Tony. I already finished!"

"Good! Agatino, do me a favor, bring me some water."

"With sugar," Aunt Carmela says. "Tony, are you all right?"

"Yes, yes, Aunt," Tony says, putting his hands on Signora Zappulla's head.

"You got something to tell me?"

Agatino comes back with the water and the sugar and gives it to Tony. Tony drinks it, sighs, and says, "I met Uncle Sal while I was buying *Vanity Fair*. He said, 'Tony, why don't you throw a nice barbecue tomorrow night and invite Nick and Mindy?'"

"Nick and Mindy?" Aunt Carmela says.

Tony nods. "Yes . . . Nick and Mindy . . . You remember Nick, don't you, Aunt?"

Aunt Carmela makes a face, *Of course.*

Tony looks at Aunt Carmela. Aunt Carmela sees into Tony's mind. Then she nods. "You deal with the hair," she says.

"But Aunt—"

"And let me think about the clothes."

"But Aunt—"

"Shut up. Please—she needs to look like a *bride*!"

UNCLE SAL WOULD REALLY
LIKE TO SEE YOU

U ncle Sal would really like to see you at the barbecue tomorrow evening. Mindy wants to introduce her fiancé Nick
Palumbo to the whole family," Tony told everyone. And
everyone has obliged. It's the fateful evening of the fateful barbecue,
and *it could well be a memorable barbecue . . . one of those barbecues
you don't think much about and then they turn out real nice . . .
elegant guests, the whole family together, music, dim lighting, the mood
carefree and intimate . . . it could be a really memorable barbecue,*
Tony thinks, standing on the stairs inside his house, from where he
can look out at the whole garden. Wearing a puffy fuchsia-colored
Indian silk shirt and a tight pair of matching pants, Tony takes a
last drag on his third menthol cigarette of the day, then walks out
into the garden to greet Uncle Sal's copywriter, the *americano* who
got food poisoning from eating amaretti.

"Are you sure I'm repulsive enough?" Mindy asks Aunt Carmela in
a corner of the garden.

Mindy is wearing one of those dresses her mother makes her from a pattern, chosen for the occasion by Aunt Carmela: puffed sleeves, crochet work, lace trimmings. On top of her head, a back-combed bridal hairdo so big there's enough hair for four women.

"Don't worry, Mindy," Aunt Carmela says. "I know men."

Aunt Carmela invented a brilliant method to remain a spinster: to dress up as a bride *before* getting married, that way men get an eyeful of what they're likely to end up with, and they take off and never come back.

When Mindy first suspected that Uncle Sal had killed her father, she decided to remain a spinster, too: she wasn't sure that Uncle Sal was really guilty, but, thinking about it, she reached the conclusion that, even if he wasn't guilty, he might be guilty, and she didn't want to have anything to do with a world in which there was a possibility your mother's brother might have killed your father. "Aunt, I forgive all of them," she said one day, "but I want to stay single, because if I get married and accidentally bring a child into the world, I'll take a machine gun and make it a clean sweep."

Aunt Carmela knew Mindy wasn't joking. She'd had the same thought forty years before.

Valentina is sitting farther along the wicker couch: red lipstick, bleached linen pants, peach-colored T-shirt, matching moccasins, legs crossed, a sullen look on her face. Next to her, Rosy is busy making sure her stockings don't run. She's wriggling about, trying to find the right position, and every time she moves, her skirt rides farther up her legs.

"Fuck, who the fuck told Tony wicker was 'in'?"

"Do you always *have* to dress like some kind of Lolita whore?" Valentina says.

Rosy smiles: she loves compliments. "Listen, I told Steve I got a cousin with a broken heart. He told me if I want I can introduce you to the singer from the White Cakes. But you'd need to put on something a little more . . . more . . . Why don't you get Cinzia to lend you something?"

"Oh, sure," Valentina says, "so now I'm going to dress like a hooker, just like Cinzia does, so I can go out with the singer from the . . . White Cakes?"

"Exactly!" Rosy says. "Dressed down with combat boots, you know, unlaced."

" 'Dressed down'?"

"Sure . . . like you don't give a fuck," Rosy says, miming somebody who doesn't give a fuck, opening her legs and putting on a sulky expression.

Valentina looks straight at her. "Your panties are showing," she says.

"Fuck," Rosy says. "I fucking knew it!"

Nick is at home, looking out at the barbecue through a crack in the shutters. He's sweating in his blue graduation suit, a nylon-worsted blend. "Fuck," he says out loud. "No way am I going to this fucking barbecue. No fucking way. I'm out of here. I'm gone. I'm in . . . Honolulu. Honolulu? Why the fuck did I think of Honolulu? Maybe the fucking barbecue reminds me of Honolulu! But who the fuck's ever been to Honolulu?"

Then Nick remembers Uncle Sal stroking his cheek and saying with a smile, "Make sure you don't miss the next barbecue, eh, Nicky?" Clumsily, he knots his tie.

Coming up Via Etnea, Lou Sciortino Junior stopped in three different bars and knocked back a couple of gins in each. So by the time he sets foot in Tony's garden, he's already dead drunk, and feels like he's back on Mulberry Street at the Festival of San Gennaro! Colored balloons, colored streamers, colorfully dressed guests, men on one side, women on the other, the bandstand with the musicians in blue uniforms . . . *Now they're gonna bring out the cannoli!* he thinks.

And here's the guy from Sal Scali's photo, dressed in fuchsia like an eighties soap star!

"You must be the *americano* Uncle Sal's expecting, right?" he says. "I'm Tony, Tony, *capish?*"

"*Capisco,*" Lou says.

"Tell me," the guy from the photo says, "in America, in the original of *Baretta*, how the fuck do you translate *minchia?*"

The band has started up: *Abballate, abballate, fimmini schette e maritate . . .*

"We translate it as *fuck* . . ." Lou says.

"Oh, right," the guy from the photo says. "*Minchia* means *fuck!*"

"Sure," Lou says.

Meanwhile, nobody's dancing, but everyone's starting to clap hands in time to the music.

Uncle Sal is in the middle of the men's section with his legs apart and his hands in his pockets, swiveling his head to take in every nook and cranny of the garden like he's some kind of TV camera. When anyone says hello, he doesn't respond, just nods. And he's the only person not clapping in time to the music.

Tony pushes his way through the crowd with Lou in tow. He bows to Uncle Sal.

"Your copywriter's here!" he says.

How the fuck did they ever give birth to such an idiot? Uncle Sal thinks as he nods. Tony does a pirouette, claps his hands enthusiastically, and walks off in the direction of the grills, where Nunzio and Agatino, dressed in white, with chef's hats on their heads, are handling big slabs of Argentinian beef from the prize-winning butcher Tano Falsaperla and Sons. Nunzio picks them up with the thumb and middle finger of his right hand and passes them to Agatino, who puts them carefully on the grill, all in time to the music.

Uncle Sal looks at Lou and nods contentedly. *He's a good kid, he came on time!*

Lou passes a hand over his face and looks around, with the same childish wonder he used to feel when his grandfather used to take him to the Mulberry Street parade. A guy with a small mustache, wearing a black suit, is clapping his hands and looking at him like he wants to whack him. Some guys are dancing with their arms linked and smiling at him like they smile only in San Francisco. Another guy isn't clapping, because he's got a plate of beef in his hand, but sways his hips in time to the music, trying his best not to drop the meat.

Meanwhile, a little woman dodges an old lady the size of a wardrobe, like something out of *The Ladykillers*, and walks unsteadily toward Lou. She's carrying a tray with a bottle of gin and a glass. She looks startlingly like Arthur Scafati's crazy aunt, the one they locked in the attic whenever anybody paid them a visit in the Bronx.

"Thanks, Cettina," Uncle Sal says. "Help yourself, Lou, it's just for you."

Nick closes the door of his house. Has he forgotten anything? *Not a thing! Not a fucking thing!* He walks toward Tony's garden, his moccasins sliding strangely on the asphalt, thinking, *For fuck's sake, who is this Mindy? I've seen so many girls at Tony's barbecues, some of them were even pretty . . . But Mindy? Who the fuck is Mindy?* Nick is bad at fitting names to faces in normal circumstances, so now, you gotta be kidding! *And Tony, fuck him, he has so many fucking relatives!*

When Nick makes his entrance in the garden, Uncle Sal signals to the band, which stops playing all of a sudden. Everybody at the barbecue freezes and turns to Nick. Nick looks at everybody. Everybody looks at Nick. They're all thinking the fiancé has arrived, and they burst into applause.

Uncle Sal signals to the band again, and they resume playing.

Abballate, abballate, fimmini schette e maritate . . .

"That's him," Uncle Sal says to Lou. Lou looks around, searching for Scafati's crazy aunt. He spots her immediately, because Cettina is wearing a red dress with sequins and is the shortest person here. Lou goes up to her.

"Excuse me," he says to her, "could I have another gin, please?"

Cettina turns anxiously to a woman who's passing, who must be a relative or a friend because she clutches her arm like she's drowning.

"Mari," she says, "do you speak English? Some of my guests are foreigners and I can't understand what they're saying."

Mari looks at Lou and is about to speak when Lou says, "Thanks, I'll do it myself," and walks away.

Mari takes Cettina by the shoulders and starts shaking her. "What did he say, what did he say?"

You never know, you might miss a compliment, a few words of appreciation from a man, just because you don't know English.

————

Nick is still by the entrance, not moving. Tony joins him. "Come on," he says eagerly. "I'll take you to see Uncle Sal! He's waiting for you, Nick! Hurry up!"

"Did you know that arranged marriages cause neuroses?" Alessia says to Cinzia in a corner of the garden opposite Rosy and Valentina.

Alessia is wearing thick, light-colored cotton pants, lace-up suede ankle boots, and a man's brown sport coat, like all the girls studying psychology in Rome.

"Especially when a woman arranges a marriage herself, and allows herself to be influenced by her culture, by inherited tastes and—"

"You're talking bullshit," Cinzia interrupts. "If you arrange the marriage yourself, it's not an arranged marriage anymore . . . An arranged marriage is called an arranged marriage because you don't fucking arrange it yourself!"

Cinzia is wearing a white sleeveless top, a pair of very wide pants full of big pockets, and boots. That's how female anthropology students dress in Siena.

"Yes, but, fuck, I'm sorry for Vale . . ." Alessia says. They both turn to look at Valentina and realize Rosy's miniskirt has ridden right up her thighs.

They look at each other and run to her to make a screen.

In the meantime, Valentina is looking at Nick.

"But how can you like him?" Cinzia asks. "His face is so nondescript, no distinctive features . . ."

"Distinctive features? Who gives a fuck about distinctive features?" Valentina says.

"You're in my light," Rosy says. "I can't see a fucking thing."

Tony drags Nick to see Uncle Sal. When they reach him, Uncle Sal is looking away, toward some indeterminate spot in the garden. Then he turns abruptly to Nick, looks him straight in the eyes, stands up, grabs his neck, squeezes it like he wants to break it, and starts shaking him. "Nicky, you came! Nicky, *bello, bello!*"

Tony is moved by what he sees. Nick coughs. Uncle Sal takes his cheeks in his hands, squeezes them, and starts shaking him again. "*Bello*, let's go for a walk! I gotta introduce you to Lou. You speak English, Nicky?"

They walk arm in arm around the garden, Uncle Sal short but perfectly upright, Nick tall but bent. Uncle Sal gives him a powerful tug. "Of course you speak English, your name's Nicky!" Then a more suggestive tug. "*Minchia*, Tony told me you play the guitar. So, English . . ." A final, assertive tug. "Of course you speak it!"

They reach Lou.

"*Minchia*, Nicky, here we are. Do you like the barbecue? You really gotta come more often! Look, here's Lou! Go on, Nick, say hello to Lou!"

"*Piacere*," Nick says.

"Nice to meet you," Lou says.

"*Encantado*," Tony says, taking advantage of the opportunity to introduce himself again, in case Lou didn't understand the first time. "I'm Tony, Tony, *capito?*"

Uncle Sal looks at Tony. *What the fuck does he want? We're working here!*

Tony takes the hint. "Excuse me," he says, "but I gotta supervise the barbecue," and disappears.

Abballate, abballate, fimmini schette e maritate . . .

"Now, Nick," Uncle Sal says, "Lou is an American who writes the mottoes for my amaretti . . . *Minchia*, Nick, did you ever taste my amaretti?"

"Sure, Don Scali," Nick says. "Tony—"

"*Minchia*," Uncle Sal says to Lou, "did you hear that? He never tasted my amaretti. Incredible! Cettina, Cettina, where the fuck are you?"

Cettina appears out of nowhere, like she's been waiting just for Uncle Sal to call her.

Uncle Sal gives her a reproving but affectionate look. "Cettina, how come you never gave Nick my amaretti to taste?"

For a brief moment, Cettina looks puzzled.

"Come on, Cettina, come on," Uncle Sal says, shaking Nick by the neck, "let's remedy that right now! Bring me a big box of amaretti!"

Cettina lifts a hand to her chest and rushes off.

"So, we were saying?" Uncle Sal says. "Oh, yes, Nicky, you see Lou?" and he twists his head around so he can see better. "Lou's a foreigner . . . a foreigner! So, *minchia*, are we going to show him Catania or what? I said, are we going to show him around? Nicky, I'm talking to you!"

"Yes, yes, Don Scali, of course . . ."

"Okay, then! So tomorrow you take him around, show him the sights. Agreed, Nicky?"

"Of course, Don Scali, of course!"

"Okay, then!"

Cettina appears with a big box of amaretti.

Uncle Sal, who's tenderly squeezing Nick's neck with one hand and Lou's arm with the other, says, "Cettina, dig me one out!"

Cettina jumps. Both her hands are occupied holding the box.

"I'll hold it," Lou says.

Cettina separates one amaretto from the others and hands it to Uncle Sal.

Without even deigning to look at Nick, Uncle Sal forces it into his mouth. "So, we agreed?" he says to Lou. "Nicky'll take you around, show you the sights. You'll see the elephant, you'll see the cathedral, you'll see . . . Cettina, another amaretto . . . you'll see Via Etnea . . . But please don't let him out of your sight, you never know, you might miss something . . . You like Sal Scali's amaretti, eh, Nicky? Here! Have another!"

Then suddenly he relaxes his grip and walks off without saying goodbye, wiping the powder from his hands.

"The last time I saw Uncle Sal so affectionate," Rosy says, "was with Girolamo Santonocito, and two days later they found him in an irrigation channel at the beach, all trussed up with his dick in his mouth."

Alessia and Cinzia look at each other. They were thinking the same thing, but fuck, *not in front of Valentina*! They look at Rosy, as if to say, *Shut the fuck up*, but the damage has been done. A tear is already streaming down Valentina's right cheek.

Rosy, who doesn't understand a fucking thing of what's going on, settles on the couch.

O n the plane, Chaz is fixing a couple of martinis, one for himself and another for Frank, who immediately after a blow job from Greta always knocks back a martini. God knows why. After a blow job, Greta ought to be the one knocking back a martini!

The plane is like one of those fifties diners painted by that realist painter Frank's so crazy about . . . what's the cocksucker's name? Whenever Frank sees a painting by this painter, he always says, "Damn, it's so magical, it makes me feel sad!" Anyway, the plane has cream-colored seats and green carpeting. Leonard is sitting near the cockpit, because he doesn't like to fly and for some reason feels more comfortable up front. Chaz is fixing the two martinis at the bar, which is just behind the cockpit. Frank and Greta are at the back of the plane. At least Chaz and Leonard assume Frank's there, because from where they are, they can only see Greta, or rather, they can see her blond hair and her eyes bobbing up at more or less regular intervals (roughly every two or three seconds) above the back of the seat in front.

To avoid thinking the usual thoughts that cloud his mind whenever he sets foot on a plane (the plane hurtling downward as he faces the last seconds of his life with great dignity, his funeral, his inconsolable father and mother, the women he's known—how many? thirty, forty, sixty? amazing how you can't remember a fucking thing when you're about to croak!—anyway, the women are all there, also inconsolable, his male friends, though, not many of them, are all talking about their own concerns . . .), Leonard keeps his eyes fixed on the top of the seat above which Greta's eyes keep bobbing and he gets an idea for a short: just eyes, nothing but close-ups of eyes, the eyes of women as they're fucking, all kinds of women, in all kinds of positions. Indifferent eyes, loving eyes, disgusted eyes, amused eyes, and . . . thoughtful eyes, thoughtful like Greta's. Because right now Greta doesn't so much seem busy with a blow job as with a think job. Maybe because Frank is moaning and can't speak, and if he can't speak she can think. Or maybe it's because she's got this bee in her bonnet that Frank is using her to make *the other woman* jealous, even though she doesn't know who the fuck *the other woman* is. Or maybe it's just because the unthinkable has happened!

My God, Frank inviting her to a party in Rome! A public party—her? Sure, it's normal for somebody like Frank, when he has to go to Italy, to take a woman with him to give him blow jobs in the plane or hotel. But then he expects her to stay at the hotel, because he's ashamed to be seen with her, like when he invites you to dinner *at his house* and buys crappy Chinese food in crappy cartons, and never, never, never takes you to Bobby's restaurant in Tribeca, where he likes to boast about black hookers and scumbag pimps.

Asshole!

The day before they left, what the asshole told himself was this: *Here's how I'll play it. I'll tell her about the party so it sounds really tempting, and sooner or later, she'll ask me to take her.* In fact, Frank felt a little ridiculous, because it's absurd trying to tell a whore like Greta about a party so it sounds really tempting, because obviously she's going to find it tempting anyway. All whores find parties tempting. But he had to do it, so Greta would ask him to take her with him, then if those FBI bastards questioned him he could say, "She's the one who asked me," in front of everyone.

So he told her all the top Italian producers—De Angelis, Lombardo, Bernabei—would be at the party, *cazzarola*!

Greta still couldn't see the reason why Frank was behaving with her like this in private.

He was telling her all these things about the party, and Greta was thinking, *I already give you blow jobs anyway, and I know you're friends with these people you're talking about, you don't have to remind me.* And besides, Greta had taken her first glorious steps in the movie business with Cameron! And Cameron had become a star, and she knew why! Because she always said, "Remember, Greta, when you go out with a producer, it's not because he can give you fame and fortune! You go out with him because you're genuinely interested in him, in his personality! So please don't quiver when you hear the word 'producer'!"

Frank couldn't understand what the matter was with the whore, because for half an hour he'd been shooting off these big fucking names and she didn't react! He was going on and on about VIPs and the whore was filing her fucking nails! What the fuck was the matter with her? Was she on some kind of hand-job improvement mission? He ought to have worked on her better, given her more confidence.

Madonna, what a mess!

Then suddenly, in a blinding flash, Frank knew: he'd never get Greta to ask him to take her to Catania, no matter who was on the guest list. Never. Frank felt a very distinct spasm in his colon. But he mustered his strength and, restraining every homicidal impulse in his body, even though it was quite obvious that Greta would rather be burned alive than show any interest in that shitass party, went closer to the blond cow, stroked her cheek, and said, "Obviously, sweetheart, you're coming, too!"

"Me?"

Without so much as a shiver of excitement, Greta went to the bathroom, looking bored, even her way of walking saying, *Shit, that's all I needed now, a party,* closed the door behind her, and, once she was alone, was seized with panic.

"Me? But what am I going to wear?"

"EXCUSE ME, YOU MUST BE NICKY, AM I RIGHT?"

E xcuse me, you must be Nicky, am I right?"

At Tony's barbecue, Lou suddenly finds himself facing a large woman with an impressively wide chest, four double chins, eight dangling corollas of fat around her face, a lacquered hairdo, a shiny black dress with a big blotch across the stomach (that was Nunzio's fault, after he tried some acrobatics with one of the slabs of beef from the prizewinning butcher Tano Falsaperla and Sons), and shoes that look like fifties convertibles.

"I'm Mindy's mother," the woman says. "My brother Sal tells me you know my daughter."

It may not happen to everyone, but when you're in a state of intoxication, it can be quite pleasant to be confused with someone else. Lou nods and, dodging arms, glasses, and plates with some difficulty, follows the convertibles across the lawn.

Suddenly the convertibles stop and Lou senses the presence of a scented body. The scent isn't perfume, it's naturally occurring. He looks up and meets the eyes of a girl dressed like one of Fonzie's girlfriends, eyes it's impossible to penetrate. Eyes that say, *Don't even think about it, you asshole.*

Think about what? Lou doesn't understand. Obviously he's been thinking about something, but what? Has he acted like an asshole? But he just got here!

"*Piacere*, I'm Rosamunda," the girl says with an offended air, and walks away in the direction of Nick and Aunt Carmela.

Lou watches her as she's moving away. He doesn't understand, but he likes that offended air.

"Nicky, this is Mindy," Aunt Carmela says, giving Mindy's dress a final once-over.

"*Piacere*, I'm Rosamunda," Mindy says with a forced smile.

"*Piacere*, I'm Nick," Nick says, and thinks, *Fuck, they've already got this one decked out like a bride! But where does she come from? One of Tony's TV series?*

Nick looks around in confusion and meets Valentina's eyes. She's still sitting with Rosy on the wicker couch. Nick smiles. Valentina gets up indignantly and walks away with an offended air. Nick doesn't understand, but he likes that offended air.

Champagne! Let's toast this meeting . . . Tony's voice, raised over the high-pitched sounds of the band, echoes around the garden, and even beyond the garden, as far as the other side of the street, between the sun-yellowed tufts of grass and the dark masses of volcanic rock.

IN ROME, CECCAROLI
HAS DONE HIS JOB WELL

n Rome, Ceccaroli has done his job well. At the party after the premiere, at the Hotel Hassler Villa Medici above the Spanish Steps, the elite of Italian cinema—De Angelis, Lombardo, Bernabei, the top brass from Titanus, Medusa, Lux, socially conscious actresses, actors, and starlets, writers, committed critics, and paparazzi—really are there. If Sean hadn't canceled his suite at the Hassler only yesterday, it would have been a triumph for Ceccaroli, *a scene out of* La Dolce Vita *rewritten by him, and him alone.* Ceccaroli even managed to find, on the net, a photograph of Greta and Cameron, bare-breasted, whipping a bodybuilder, which he sent to the Roman magazines. The result is an impressive crowd of paparazzi outside the Hassler, who go wild when Frank and Greta arrive.

"Are you ashamed like Cameron, Greta?"

"Tell us about Cameron!"

"Everything *bene*," Greta says, radiant. "Rome is *bellissima*!"

Frank, who's wearing a white jacket and black tie, grips her arm tightly, to stop her talking bullshit. But then the whore goes,

"Ooooww!" and Frank thinks, *Cazzarola, the bitch has delicate skin,* before he realizes she's stumbled. He bends over to look at Greta's ankle, massages it slowly, and, trying to keep his paunch inside his white double-breasted tuxedo, says, "Did you hurt yourself, honey?"

"It's nothing, Frank," Greta says, ever more radiant.

What the fuck's the whore laughing about? Frank wonders while the paparazzi pop their flashes for all they're worth.

The fact is, Greta has a whole lot of reasons to be radiant, all these flashes mean fame and fortune, but right now fame and fortune are far down the list of things on her mind. This afternoon, inviting her to the party, Frank stroked her cheek and said . . . *Could it be? It's unbelievable . . . Is Frank really . . . falling in love with her?*

Frank feels Greta's arm tightening around his. *What are you doing squeezing my arm, you whore?* But you've got to put a brave face on things. He squeezes her arm, too, and looks at her.

Greta's eyes are shining. And just then, a thought comes into her little head, a thought that, at least once in her life, comes into the little head of every Greta in the world. *But is this what I really want? To be like Cameron and Charlize? Do I really want a villa in Beverly Hills and a penthouse on Fifth Avenue? Or do I want nothing but to have this little man take me away with him to a cottage in the country, with me watching from the kitchen window while he cuts firewood, him maybe stroking my belly when I'm pregnant?*

As all inveterate seducers, pimps, and users of every species know, there's nothing in the world easier than making a woman like Greta—or any woman—believe you love her.

When they enter the lobby of the Hassler, Ceccaroli comes up to them. He's looking nervous.

"For the seating, Frank, my idea was—"

"Ceccarò, I'm sure your idea's fine," Frank says. "Did you put Greta on my right or on my left?"

After years of dinners and parties of every kind, Ceccaroli knows a thing or two about etiquette, and was thinking of putting Greta next to the famous left-wing critic, opposite Frank. Now he immediately says, "Of course, Frank, Greta's on your right."

On the seventh floor, in the Rooftop Restaurant, Frank, who'd like to hurry things along, is forced to shake hundreds of sweaty hands. A real bullshit artist, with a face as red as a beet, perfectly groomed white hair, and a shiny blue tie, starts busting his balls about the view, the Spanish Steps, the Pantheon, St. Peter's, Eisenhower, the Queen of England. Then Frank has a brilliant idea. "Thank you," he says, "but I already know all about the Hassler, my friend John Gotti told me about it ten years ago, he was here for two weeks." It takes just three seconds, *cazzarola*, for the bullshit artist to disappear.

All the important Italians—de Angelis, Bernabei, the people from Titanus, Medusa, and Lux—are at the table, along with Leonard, who's sitting opposite Frank, an Italian woman writer with a pissed-off face, her actor-director husband, the famous critic, an unwashed guy with dirty glasses, the woman president of the jury for a literary prize, an old lady who keeps asking Greta, "Would you like some water, dear? Are you tired, dear?" and the dear herself, who's radiant, eating a plate of pasta in front of Frank for the first time: *scialatelli* from Sorrento with seafood sauce and zucchini flowers.

Looking at his crystal glass, covered in oily fingerprints, Frank realizes he's getting nervous. The *macaronis*, the whore, the old woman, the unwashed critic, and all this bullshit about getting Greta to ask him to take her to Catania: everything's starting to get on his nerves!

"Do you know why I like your work?" He's distracted from his somber thoughts by the unwashed critic's thin little voice. The critic has decided the moment has come to say a few banalities to Leonard Trent, just to show they did the right thing inviting him. "Because you have no professional anxieties. It's obvious after seeing *Plastic Love* that you're driven by a single fixed idea: that the cinema exists and is therefore something that can simply be possessed, grabbed hold of, something you can enter, something that can and must be learned . . . But that's what genuine cinema always is, in every era . . . a revolt against the privileges of cinematic dynasties. Take De Sica. What do you think drove De Sica? Ideological concerns? No, simply the desire to see the birth and death of a few images and ideas worthy of birth and death."

I'd like to see your birth and death, Leonard thinks, forcing himself to smile like he's grateful for the praise.

Pleased with himself, the unwashed critic then decides to fulfill the evening's other obligation: to say a few words to the Jayne Mansfield type on his left.

"Do you like De Sica?" he asks Greta, smiling and showing her his yellow teeth with pieces of zucchini flower still stuck in them.

Greta, who's thinking about the steamed king prawns with Sicilian couscous, the mozzarella, and the buffalo ricotta she's finally going to eat with Frank at Babbo in the West Village, where Frank is sure to take her now, answers without hesitation, "Delicious. I went to Da Sica's in Tribeca with Drew and Quentin. A really hip restaurant."

The unwashed critic is puzzled for a moment, then casually takes off his dirty glasses and polishes them on a corner of the tablecloth. Frank swallows with difficulty. He'd like to slap Greta: it wouldn't be the first time he slapped a woman in public. But instead, he decides to laugh, softly at first, then in that loud, vulgar way Italians expect from Italian-Americans at table and in public.

They all laugh, of course, especially the old lady from the prize jury, who says, "You know, dear, when I was your age I often went to a trattoria called Da Sica's. But that was in Naples . . ."

Frank can feel himself getting more and more nervous. He hates the old lady, the unwashed critic and the whore, hates the writer, too, and her dickhead husband, hates those cheapskate Italian producers, hates that asshole Leonard who's smiling like a faggot. Reacting to a really painful spasm in his colon, he decides he might as well destroy himself with wine, then at the last moment changes his mind and decides to destroy the whore instead, and fills her glass to the brim. *Delicious, huh? Here: drink, bitch, drink!*

Then he has a sudden flash, an illumination.

"In my opinion," he says, turning to the unwashed critic, "one of the greatest Italian directors is Franco Zeffirelli. Have you seen *Sparrow*? Images worthy of birth and . . . you know, like you said."

"Aesthetic kitsch . . ." the pissed-off woman writer says.

"What?" Frank says.

"Well . . ." the unwashed critic says, "I don't know if Zeffirelli is exempt from the privileges of cinematic dynasties . . . He owes everything to Visconti, and—"

"Zeffirelli is one of our greatest geniuses," Bernabei says and, to save the situation, raises his glass of wine.

"Bravo Zeffirella!" Greta says, raising her glass, which is full to the brim, and almost emptying it on the snow-white tablecloth.

"Long live Zeffirella!" Leonard says, also raising high his glass, with an amused look on his face.

"Absolutely!" Frank says, his round eyes fixed on Greta's laughing blue eyes. "They ought to show *Sparrow* in film schools . . . it's a moving love story against the magnificent . . . magnificent . . . backdrop of the Catanese baroque. An emotional epic, a hymn to passion set in that splendid Sicilian city! In that street . . . What the hell's the name of that street?"

"The one with the convent?" the old lady says.

"Exactly," Frank says, "that street full of churches and works of art, with that gallery thing joining the two wings of the convent . . ." Frank mimes the two wings with a flapping motion of his arms.

"The Bridge of the Sparrow," the old lady says, looking into Greta's blue eyes with her own dull gray eyes. "A rendezvous for lovers even today."

"Exactly," Frank says, exhausted.

Greta places her hand on Frank's forearm, sighs, weakens, thinks, *Why is the world so unfair and yet so beautiful sometimes, so full of . . . longing?* and says, "Will you take me there, Frank?"

"Where?" Frank asks, with the same radiant expression he had on that long-ago day when, as a child, he beat up Carmine Cacace's son, who was three years older than him and was always tormenting him.

"The Bridge of the Sparrow," Greta whispers.

"Of course, sweetheart!" Frank says.

ON THE BEACH AT MARZAMEMI
TWO TOURISTS ARE READING

On the beach at Marzamemi two tourists are reading, lying on chaise longues. It's obvious they're tourists, because they're reading. It's obvious Don Lou Sciortino has just finished eating, because he's drinking Brancamenta. He's sitting under a canopy where there are four tables with red checkered paper tablecloths. His table is still a mess. But Don Mimmo arrives quickly to clear it, rolling the tablecloth into a ball along with all the crumbs. Don Lou Sciortino nods. He's looking at a reinforced concrete scaffolding, an ominous sign. They've started to build even here. The earth movers and the bricklayers have already moved in. In New York, these things were the basis of Don Lou Sciortino's fortune. But here in Marzamemi he wouldn't even build a doll's house for Don Mimmo's little granddaughter. There's a small island opposite the beach of Marzamemi, with a beautiful villa on it. Whenever Don Lou thought about Marzamemi in America, he thought about Don Mimmo's little restaurant, La Tonnara, and about the villa on the island. In his mind they were the only buildings that existed. The smallest change, and Marzamemi would become like any other place.

"Who?" Pippino asks. He's known as 'U Ciantru, the Oleander, because he's as poisonous as an oleander, a plant it's best to keep away from donkeys and horses. A real expert with a knife, Pippino. In Catania, forty years ago, everybody called him 'U Nivuro, the black man, because they said he had a black heart, nobody trusted him anymore, he didn't lick anybody's ass. People said the only thing Pippino licked was the blade of his knife, but what he actually did was rub soap onto it to help it slide in easier and make the wounds burn more. One day about forty years ago, Don Lou Sciortino took Pippino aside, bought him a Fernet, down in Turi Cricuocu's bar, and said, "They tell me you're black, but to me you're like an oleander. Poisonous, sure. But my grandfather taught me you can plant oleanders in a garden, tend them, and water them." Don Lou Sciortino's grandfather was right. Result: forty years later Pippino is still at Don Lou Sciortino's side, and everybody, in Sicily and America, calls him Don Lou's *ciantru*.

"The guy who lived on that island," Don Lou says, jutting his chin in the direction of the little island.

Pippino is dressed in a brown suit from a department store, but he looks neater than a lot of people who have their clothes made to measure. He's got a bald skull, a round face, and an aquiline nose. He isn't tall. To look at him, you'd take him for a French choreographer, one of the few who aren't gay. Under his jacket, he's wearing a black polo shirt buttoned to the neck.

"Vitaliano Brancati," Pippino says.

"Right," Don Lou says.

Don Lou Sciortino retired Pippino ten years ago. Pippino lives alone in a very clean apartment, and goes on self-improving vacations, spending whole weeks in the most exclusive apartment hotels in the world, reading books.

"What's Brancati like?"

"Good," Pippino says.

"Shall we go?" Don Lou says, looking at his watch.

Pippino leaps to his feet and looks along the boardwalk. "Whenever you like, sir."

The Jaguar bumps over the dirt road. On either side, dry walls of very white stone beneath carob trees and prickly pear. Pippino parks in a patch of open ground full of the carcasses of agricultural machinery, tractor tires, lead drums. Two dogs tied to a cart snarl at them. A shabby-looking young man is trying to repair a rototiller in front of a building made out of blocks of concrete, with slabs of fibrocement for a roof. The young man drops the rototiller and wipes his hands, first on a dishrag, and then on his pants. He says, "They told me you need prickly pear. You can get all you want around here."

Don Lou and Pippino look at him in silence, then walk slowly toward the olive grove opposite the patch of ground, until Pippino spots the manhole. It's open. Pippino makes a move like he's going in, but Don Lou stops him with a look that says, *No, I gotta go first.* Don Lou stoops to avoid banging his head. He hesitates a moment on the narrow steps and Pippino supports him, very gently and tenderly. The air-conditioning is on full strength. Jacobbo Maretta is wearing blue Bermudas and a juice-stained undershirt.

People say Jacobbo Maretta doesn't exist, that he's just an invention of Lillo Virtude, who's in Ucciardone Prison but wants people to think he's got a man on the outside. An official FBI report a while ago said he died when a motorboat sank with some Cuban businessmen on board. The whole thing stank, though. Who the fuck has ever seen a Cuban businessman? Lots of people think Jacobbo Maretta is alive and kicking, which in fact he is.

In fact, to be more specific, here's what happened: a few months before going into Ucciardone, Virtude made sure that Maretta disappeared, and spread a whole lot of contradictory rumors about his disappearance. "I need somebody on the outside. I need you."

Now Maretta lives in this underground bunker in the countryside inland from Marzamemi. Whenever he has to go out, he takes a tractor as far as the village, where a yellow Fiat 127 is waiting to take him to a dealer in garden statues in Ispica. There he gets on a truck, changes inside it, and when he gets out, usually at Catania Airport, he's all spruced up.

"Don Lou, you really must forgive me! I haven't been out in three months, I'm turning into an animal." Jacobbo Maretta has thick hair dyed jet-black and what looks like a fake mustache. "Pippino! Still kicking?"

Pippino's only response is to look at Don Lou. Don Lou nods to Pippino, and Pippino nods to Maretta.

"*Minchia*, they broke the mold when they made you," Maretta says. "Pippino, you must do me a personal courtesy. I know you like getting laid, so do Jacobbo a favor: make some babies! We need more people like you!" Maretta sighs. "Don Lou, you did the right thing coming to Sicily. How's your grandson? He's a good kid, just like his grandpa . . . Oh, by the way, Don Lou, I wanted to ask your advice . . . It'll soon be time to plant beans . . . But you know what happens? They dry up on me! The other year my beans dried up! So how can I be sure now? It's expensive, you know, I gotta hire men to plant them, I gotta put in irrigation, water pipes . . . It's one expense after another . . . One's thing's for sure, agriculture ain't what it used to be . . . Fuck it, we got unions now! The men arrive on time and leave on time . . . and fuck, the money they make . . . So you know what I say? Even if I've got just one broken bean—one *fava rotta*, you know what I mean?—it isn't worth the effort! I don't like these beans, they're small, they're sad, they don't ripen . . . I don't trust beans anymore! Zucchini, now, they're beautiful . . . You eat pasta with zucchini and *ricotta salata* at Don Mimmo's? *Minchia*, Don Mimmo is still Don Mimmo!"

"Don Mimmo seemed fine to me," Don Lou says. "Sure, he's getting old, like the rest of us, but you can trust him. His hand shakes a little when he brings the food, but you can still trust him."

"And Pippino, what did Pippino eat? Don't tell me, I know: *spaghetti alla pescatora* with a whole fucking lot of red chilies. By the way, what can I offer you? Of course, you just ate . . . Ah, how about some amaretti? I don't know, though . . . I've had this box here a long time . . . What do you think? Did they go bad? In my opinion, yes . . . These amaretti are stale! Forget it, let's get rid of these amaretti . . . Let's just get rid of them," Maretta says, and throws away the box of amaretti with an angry, disgusted gesture. "But you're going to Catania now, right? That's good! Don Lou, please, you gotta go see Sonnino. Trust me. I've seen a lot of *picciotti* who've made their way in the world. But there's nobody else I can recommend like a son. In Catania, you gotta ask after Sonnino, you gotta send for him. Because if you need somebody you can trust, I recommend this Sonnino personally."

"Jacobbo, it was a pleasure seeing you."

"What are you talking about, Don Lou? You know what an honor this was for me. So if you'll allow me . . ." Maretta takes Don Lou's hand, kneels, and kisses it.

"Get up, Jacobbo, this time I'm the one who owes you."

As they bump along the dirt road, Don Lou is lost in thought. Pippino looks straight in front of him. "You know what I think,

Pippino? Maretta's starting to look just like that actor I like . . . what's his name?"

"Charles Bronson," Pippino says.

"That's the one!" Don Lou says, and smiles.

Pippino smiles, too.

GIORGINO FAVAROTTA'S OLDER BROTHER, LEOLUCA FAVAROTTA

Giorgino Favarotta's older brother, Leoluca Favarotta, who was killed at the age of thirty-seven in a restaurant called La Paglia while eating spaghetti with cuttlefish ink (his face ended up in the plate and when they lifted it, it looked like the Saracen in a Sicilian puppet play), was the person Sal Scali really idolized. Always well dressed (he wore impeccable Irish linen suits even in summer), Leoluca Favarotta was a handsome guy and a great pool player.

Whenever he played at the Eden Pool Hall, a small crowd of fans would gather, among them Sal Scali, who was a child at the time. This was in 1949–50, when people were starting to like American games and drinks, and a pool hall was a magical place to a kid like Sal.

And now, fifty-four years later, on a day like today when he's got important decisions to make, where is Sal Scali? At the Eden Pool Hall, in the same room, on the now-rickety mezzanine, where Leoluca Favarotta used to run the table.

Of course, a lot of time has passed since then, and the felts are more yellow than green. The big painted wooden SAMBUCA signs on the walls are almost illegible, the figures on them faded: women in white dresses with parasols and gentlemen with mustaches who flirt with them, frozen forever in an image of lively chatter fueled by alcohol. The rims of these signs are full of dead flies. The manager is dozing behind a small table at the entrance. Behind him, a humming Coca-Cola machine converted to hold beer.

Uncle Sal, who's wearing a dark blue linen suit, just spoke with Frank Erra, who landed in Catania a few hours ago and immediately took refuge in the most expensive suite at the Central Palace Hotel.

Tuccio took out the cell phone, removed the SIM card, and replaced it with one of those clones with the telephone numbers of Moroccans who pick tomatoes in Pachino, then dialed the number Uncle Sal gave him and asked to speak to Frank Erra. When Chaz answered, "Hello?" at the other end, Tuccio passed the cell phone to Uncle Sal.

"This is Sal Scali," Uncle Sal said. "Is Frank Erra there?"

"Wait," Chaz said, polite as ever.

"Hello, Frank Erra here," Frank said.

"This is Sal Scali," Uncle Sal repeated. "Pleased to meet you, at least over the phone. I've heard good things about you from friends."

"Likewise. When should we meet?"

"That's just it. I think maybe not right away . . . Maybe you'd like to see a bit of Catania first. But if you want to let me know where you're planning to go, I can prepare the ground, maybe tell some of my *picciotti* to put themselves at your disposal."

Cazzarola! Frank thought. *These guys are professionals!*

"Good idea," he said. "I think I'm going to see the Bridge of the Sparrow, a friend of mine insists . . . She's a woman, you know how it is . . ."

"Sure! You got to show your friend the Bridge of the Sparrow in Catania. Or maybe your friend has some things to show you!"

Frank laughed. "See you later, Sal!" he said.

"Your health, Frank," Uncle Sal said.

Whenever he administers the last rites to someone, Uncle Sal always says, "Your health." And when he says it, Tuccio and Nuccio laugh excessively, almost hysterically, because it's often their job to bid farewell to the designated person. Uncle Sal, though, keeps his cool, just like Leoluca Favarotta, because even this "Your health" thing was something Uncle Sal got from Leoluca Favarotta, who, one day in '49, at the Eden Pool Hall, after somebody dared to address him disrespectfully, saying, "What are you doing tonight, Leoluca, you going to show me another of your tricks?," bought the guy a Strega, then said, "Your health," and finally slapped his face very hard five times, three times on one side and twice on the other.

Nuccio is laughing now, excitedly. He keeps repeating over and over, "*Minchia*, we're even killing *americani* now!"

Maria, he really likes being at the Eden Pool Hall! With his well-dressed, nice-smelling boss who tells him what the fuck he has to do, and Tuccio just as determined and professional as him, *minchia*, the two of them are like two Japanese!

TA-TANG! Nuccio cocks his well-oiled pistol to make sure everything's in working order.

Uncle Sal looks him in the eyes, coldly. "Make sure you don't fuck this up," he says. "The *americano*'s an idiot who signed his own death sentence. In business, if you make a mistake . . . you gotta pay." Frank didn't make any fucking mistake, except maybe agreeing to run Starship Pictures, but to Uncle Sal now it seems like a justified reproach.

Tuccio swallows, he's got a guilty conscience over that mess with the sergeant.

Nuccio says, "*Minchia*, we're even killing *americani* now!"

"What mistake did he make?" Tuccio says, scared.

"Shall we get to work?" Uncle Sal says.

Tuccio and Nuccio nod. They're ready. Uncle Sal nods.

"Now," Uncle Sal says, turning to Tuccio. "Nuccio takes care of the *americano* and the whore who's with him. The more damage he does, the better. After which," he says to Nuccio, handing him a rifle, "—I want you to use this rifle, not the gun—after which you bring it to me at the amaretti shop. And come right away, not like the other times . . . *capito*?"

"Sure," Nuccio says. "Whatever you say, sir."

"Good," Uncle Sal says. "In the meantime, Tuccio, you go to Sonnino's house and tell him I want to talk to him. If he asks you what about, tell him you don't know. Let's see if we can't take care of that asshole Sonnino at the same time, too."

And because you've always got to send two people when you send a message to the boss of a district, Uncle Sal adds, "Take Nunzio Aliotro with you."

AT SCALI'S AMARETTI, SIGNORINA NISCEMI IS TALKING ON THE PHONE

t Scali's Amaretti, Signorina Niscemi is talking on the phone when Pippino and Don Lou appear outside the glass and brass door.

"Yes . . . yes . . . I'm wearing the mini . . . the denim one with the daisies and the slits . . . Right . . . right . . . With the high heels . . . I almost cracked my head open leaving home this morning . . . Is it short? When I sit down, you can see everything . . . Shut up, shut up, somebody's coming in . . . shut up, I said . . . I'll call you later. Later . . ."

Signorina Niscemi hangs up, looks around, crosses her legs, settles, says, "Fuck . . ." stands up, gets a few sheets of bonded paper, returns to her chair, sits down again, crosses her legs again, settles again.

Pippino comes in, followed at a short distance by Don Lou. *Two men, one a bit . . . mature, the other with a nice face but just about ready to meet his maker,* Signorina Niscemi thinks, thrusting her big breasts forward and wriggling about on her chair. But as soon as she sees the faces of Pippino and Don Lou, the faces of people who could send *you* to meet your maker, she composes herself and picks up the sheets of bond paper. "Hello," she says. "This paperwork's driving me crazy. Makes me feel so hot . . ."

"*Buongiorno*," Pippino says. "Where is Signor Sciortino?"

"Signor Sciortino is here . . . I'm sorry, who should I say . . ."

"Tell Signor Sciortino that Don Lou Sciortino is here," Pippino says.

Signorina Niscemi picks up the telephone and dials a number. "Hello?" she says. "Your name is Lou Sciortino, right? . . . What do you mean, why? Because there's another Lou Sciortino here . . . Oh, okay, fine.

"Go ahead," she says to Pippino. "Second floor on the left."

Pippino looks at Don Lou. Don Lou nods and starts climbing the wooden staircase, hesitantly but with a very straight back.

Pippino stays put, next to a circular display case, in which an amaretto is rotating on a silver platter, to the strains of a Strauss waltz.

"What the fuck's that?" Don Lou says as he enters Lou's office. Don Lou can see perfectly well that what Lou is holding behind the desk is a crossbow, but asking the question helps him not to be overcome with emotion at seeing his grandson again.

"A crossbow," Lou says, wrapping it up in newspaper and putting it back on the desk, before going to his grandfather and kissing him.

"That's right, put it away, those contraptions are dangerous! Arthur Gelli's wife went crazy after reading a book, *Zen and Archery*, *Zen and the Art of Archery*, some crap like that, and killed her husband by mistake with one of those fucking things . . ."

"Grandpa, you just sat down, already you're talking about accidents!"

"Don't joke, Lou, I'm very angry!"

Don Lou tries to rise from the chair, can't manage it, curses, and breathes hard until he calms down.

"Can I talk in this fucking place?"

"Don't worry, Grandpa, I checked for bugs."

"I went to Marzamemi and Jacobbo made it clear to me we got to change our friends. 'I don't trust these *fave rotte* anymore,' he said, and then, 'Get rid of the amaretti.' Fuck, if we were in New York, I'd send Pippino to bring me Giorgino Favarotta, and I'd say to Giorgino, 'Giorgino, your brother did right getting shot, otherwise he'd have had to keep on living with people like you,' and then I'd shoot him myself, even though the bastard doesn't deserve to rejoin his family. As for Sal Scali, fuck, I'd tell Pippino I want him good and dead, in the morgue, with the autopsy already done, nice and cold and clean, without his intestines, and with a label on his big toe, lying there still and stiff like a fish. But we're in Sicily, Lou. The *americani* can't do shit here. In '43, even Don Vitone and Max Magnani had to sit in a corner and take orders from Pippino Russo and Vanni Sacco. Luckily, those idiots in the U.S. Army put Max in charge of storing pharmaceuticals, including morphine, *minchia*! And Don Vitone got involved in the black market, supplying bread, oil, sugar, and coffee for the Army. But both of them always respected the boss. Because you see, Lou, you always got to respect the boss! Here, we gotta respect Virtude! If Virtude tells us to stick our dicks in terra-cotta jars, we stick our dicks in terra-cotta jars, if he tells us we gotta go see some pharmacist and make him pay protection, we go see that pharmacist and make him pay protection, but if he doesn't tell us shit, we can't do shit. You see, Lou, me, Jacobbo, Virtude, La Bruna, Favarotta, Sal Scali, and even that idiot, what the fuck's his name . . . Erra, Frank Erra . . . we're organic matter, Lou, we're living organisms, and, like all living organisms, we sometimes need to lose a few cells in order to regenerate. Now, *minchia*, all we gotta do is work out which fucking cells to lose!"

"You see this grafting knife with the mother-of-pearl handle, Grandpa?" Lou says, pointing at his desk.

"My legs may not work, Lou, but I still got my sight, so yes, I can see it fine . . . But what the fuck is it got to do with anything?"

"Because of this knife, I ended up with that crossbow and three hundred euros."

"What did you do, rob a gun shop?"

"Much worse! I threatened some poor old guy in a store!"

Don Lou tries again to get up from his chair, and can't manage it. He starts swearing, and it's hard for him to calm down. "And can you tell me why you did such a fucking idiotic thing?" he asks breathlessly.

"Sal Scali asked me to. He told me to go scare the old man to keep him from squealing. A friend of his nephew Tony did an armed robbery in the old guy's store and whacked a cop."

"*Minchia!* And Sal Scali sent my grandson to do these things? Weren't there any *picciotti* that could do his business for him?"

"He told me he had to send me."

"What did it have to do with you?"

"He told me if I didn't do it, I'd be showing disrespect."

"Fuck him! He was the one showing disrespect, making you do that. You were his guest!"

Don Lou pounds the arm of the chair with his fist, curses, tries again to stand, succeeds this time, and walks three times around the room.

"Frank Erra comes to Catania, and Sal Scali makes my grandson do this fucking idiotic thing . . . after an armed robbery!"

"Frank Erra's in Catania?"

"Sure, he's already at the Central Palace Hotel, with a *picciotto*, a whore, and Leonard Trent! And I'm convinced Sal Scali already knows."

"Let's take out Sal Scali, then. Eh, Grandpa? Let's lose a few cells!"

"Lou, Lou . . . You didn't understand a fucking thing I said! Right now all we can do is talk. Phone the bastard and tell him your grandfather would like to have a few words with his excellency at the Central Palace Hotel. Then find out where Sonnino is. *Minchia*, we watch our backs, we'll come out okay!"

Meanwhile, downstairs, Signorina Niscemi is bringing Pippino his coffee. She holds the tray up near her breasts, to give Pippino something nice to look at. Pippino takes the cup, but keeps his eyes fixed on a small display case in which a miniature Sicilian cart adorned with beautiful figurines of the paladins of France, and loaded with Scali's amaretti, is endlessly turning. *Over here,* Signorina Niscemi thinks, *I'm over here,* but Pippino's a lost cause and she walks back to her chair near the door.

THIS MORNING CETTINA
WOKE WITH A START

This morning Cettina woke with a start, and very nearly banged her head on the wall. It's always the same, ever since she's been married to Tony.

The days immediately following a barbecue are usually even worse than the barbecue itself, because there's always a lot of cleaning up to do.

At the fair in Messina, Tony bought a kind of fold-up canopy, which he calls the Arab tent, and after the barbecue he has it set up in the garden and fills it full of cushions, hookahs, and bells, because according to Tony the Sicilians inherited their sense of hospitality from the Arabs—in fact, for the Arabs guests and horses were sacred. He's so sure of this that one night he woke up suddenly, and with his eyes wide open said to Cettina, "Cettina, don't you think we ought to invite some horses?" Then he went back to sleep.

In the days immediately following the barbecue, never at the barbecue, thank God, Tony even hires a caterer. And to make himself heard by the waiters while he receives his guests in the Arab tent he uses a whistle.

That's why Cettina was woken this morning by the sound of a whistle.

Cettina gets up and searches for her slippers. Then she goes out in the garden, wearing her dressing gown with the hole, her feet in slippers, her hair a mess.

Tony has put on his caftan and his pointed shoes with his initials on them.

One of the waiters passes Cettina, wearing a white jacket that's too tight and carrying a tray of Turkish coffee.

Cettina has become convinced that waiters with homosexual tendencies all end up in catering because restaurants don't want them. If a waiter's got homosexual tendencies, she figures, he might upset the customers. What she doesn't know is that Tony does the casting for the waiters himself.

The waiter places the tray in front of Tony, bending just a tad too gracefully. Next to Tony sit Felice Romano, the mechanic, in his Greek pants and a little blouse Cettina could swear she's seen on his wife, and Angelo Colombo, the dressmaker, in pearl-gray pants, a blue double-breasted jacket with gold buttons, and a yachtsman's white cap.

When Tony sees Cettina, he leaps to his feet, throws himself on her, takes her by the arm, and pulls her into the kitchen.

There's dance music playing in the kitchen, and three more waiters are swaying in time to the music, their arms in the air, as they make coffee.

Tony whispers something in her ear. In reply, Cettina lifts her arms, too, and sways in time to the music to make them understand that the music is too loud and she can't hear a fucking thing.

Tony looks at the kitchen, nods, takes her arm again, and pulls her into the living room. He closes the door and says, "What in fuck's name do you think you're doing, behaving like this? You think it's right to come into the Arab tent looking like you just escaped from a nuthouse?"

"Well, you never know. Felice and Angelo have never seen me in my house clothes!"

Tony starts to move his hands about close to his ear like he's fanning himself. Cettina thinks, *Holy shit, now he's going to lose his temper.* But Tony doesn't lose his temper.

Cettina looks at him. Tony has already got his first menthol cigarette of the day between his fingers. He lights it to calm himself down and looks out at the garden.

Where did he get that cigarette?

Tony makes a face like a puppeteer at work. "*Minchia*, Cettina," he says, "I'm a genius!"

Cettina raises her eyes to heaven.

Tony sits down in the armchair and crosses his legs. "So," he says, "Uncle Sal has gotten it into his head to fix Mindy up with Nick. And we know," he continues, uncrossing his legs and crossing them again in the other direction, "not only does Mindy not give a fuck about Nick, but Valentina's crazy about him." Tony flicks ash in the air. Cettina drags herself to the other armchair, but no sooner has she sat down than Tony stands up, goes to the sideboard, and leans against it.

"Now, you, Cettina—no offense—don't know what the fuck's going on here. But I tell you, at the barbecue, Mindy was making eyes at the *americano*."

Making eyes! Fuck, she was eating him alive!

"And the *americano* was paying just as much attention to Mindy."

Attention? He was giving her an X-ray and an ultrasound, too, for good measure.

"That's why . . ." Tony says, "that's why, although I know you don't get it, your husband, being a genius, like I just said, can show you what's going on."

Cettina has no time to say, *Don't do anything idiotic*, because Tony has already grabbed the telephone. "Signorina Niscemi," he says, "pass me the *americano*."

Cettina shakes her head. She's not even listening to him when he says, "This is Tony, Signor Sciortino . . . Tony. You remember? Can I invite you to a barbecue Sunday night?"

Cettina is still staring into space when Tony comes back and sits down, with a big smile on his face.

What a fool he is sometimes.

"So," Tony says, "Sunday night, the last big barbecue of the season! Let's see if we can't get a nice little Sicilian-American fraternization going here, and present Uncle Sal with a *fait accompli*!"

"Sure, and then Uncle Sal will make sure the *americano* disappears, and Nick has to marry Mindy because she's pregnant . . ." Cettina says.

"No, my darling wife," Tony says, "because we make sure Valentina goes off with Nick, and Uncle Sal can't do a fucking thing about it because he doesn't want to end up with a widowed niece! But right now I want you to get dressed and then you come back to the Arab tent."

UNCLE SAL HAS ARRIVED AT
THE EDEN POOL HALL

U ncle Sal has arrived at the Eden Pool Hall wearing a light gray worsted suit the tailor's just sent him five months after it was ordered. Pavone wanted to make him something a little bit fruity, with gathered sleeves ("just the thing on a light-colored suit"). Uncle Sal let him do it, and when it was ready he looked at himself in the mirror and even liked the gathering at the shoulders. Then he imagined himself walking along Via Etnea dressed that way, and changed his mind.

But now, at the Eden Pool Hall, Uncle Sal's in a very good mood. His new suit, he thinks, fits him like a glove. Sitting in his armchair on the mezzanine, he makes slow, sweeping movements with his arms the way sharp dressers do.

"Sure you don't want me to go with you, boss?" Tuccio says.

"Certain," Uncle Sal says, smiling.

Then, because he's in such a good mood and feeling talkative, he adds, "Officially, this is a social visit, so I can't show up with a *picciotto*."

Tuccio, though, makes a face, like someone who can't shrug off his doubts.

"Why the face?" Uncle Sal asks. When Uncle Sal's got his own reasons to be in a good mood, he doesn't like having them second-guessed.

"It's just that . . . if you ask me . . . it's just my opinion . . . old Sciortino has smelled a rat."

"A rat? Fuck him, he can smell a fucking zoo!"

"Smell a zoo?"

"Wake up, Tuccio! You need a kick up your ass! We're gonna fuck the grandson. Now the grandpa's here we fuck him, too!"

"Yes, but why do you think the grandpa sent for you?"

"What do you want me to say? I think he's planning to threaten me."

"What? And you want to show up without *picciotti*?"

"Sure! I'm acting in good faith!" Uncle Sal says, making a conspiratorial face, like he's saying, *I've got it all worked out.* "It's like they say in Rome, *You make a silent fart, only your ass is the wiser.* If I show up with my *picciotti* it means I got something on my conscience. Instead of which, I show up like an old friend, and as soon as the guy threatens me I give him a surprised look, like this!"

Uncle Sal opens his mouth and arms wide and gives a surprised look.

In the suite at the Central Palace Hotel, where Don Lou is waiting for him with Pippino, Uncle Sal enters with his arms open wide and a smile on his face.

"Don Lou, Don Lou! What an immense pleasure this is for me, what a wonderful surprise!"

"Give me some more wine, my throat's dry," Don Lou says to Pippino.

Sitting in a red leather armchair, without looking up at Uncle Sal, Don Lou coughs, then grabs the glass of white wine and says, still turned to the Oleander, "You see this dickhead who just arrived? We should cut his throat open, then he'll really smile, and seeing as how he's such a sharp dresser, we should pull his tongue out and let it hang there like a tie, I'll even put a nice Windsor knot in it with my own bare hands. But I'm an idiot, so I'll talk to him."

Uncle Sal feels like he's been slapped in the face. He was expecting it but not so abruptly . . . He sits down very slowly, with a surprised look on his face.

"Don Lou . . . What is it? What happened? Tell me, tell me! You're scaring me!"

"What the fuck is all this about you sending my grandson to sort out your business?"

Uncle Sal runs his fingers through his hair, then slams the fist of his right hand into the palm of his left. "Listen to me, Don Lou, listen . . . They been screwing everything up. That asshole Sonnino is busting my balls . . . and then Nicky . . . my future son-in-law . . . did that stupid thing at Uncle Mimmo's! What was I supposed to do . . . what was I supposed to do? You understand, right? I couldn't send one of my *picciotti* . . . I don't trust them. I got the feeling one of them's a rat . . . I was convinced your grandson was the only one . . . the only one! So he did it, and God bless him for it!"

"And what's Frank Erra doing in Catania?"

"Who?"

"Frank Erra, that dickhead the La Brunas put in my grandson's place."

"Who?"

Don Lou looks up slowly at Pippino.

"*Minchia!* Frank Erra!" Uncle Sal says, slapping himself hard on the forehead. "Sure! The guy the La Brunas put in your grandson's place . . . What's he doing in Catania?"

"Listen, here's the deal," Don Lou says, still looking at the Oleander. "I'm on vacation here in Catania, so I'm taking a few days to look around, I'm going to the fair, I'm going to San Giovanni li Cuti, I'm going wherever the fuck I want. But if anything happens, I won't ask any questions, I'm gonna . . . Well, do we understand each other?"

"You're doing the right thing, Don Lou! You're doing the right thing!"

"As far as I'm concerned, you can go!"

"About this Frank Erra, Don Lou," Uncle Sal says, standing up. "You want I should put somebody on his tail? Eh?"

"I said, as far as I'm concerned, you can go."

"Sure, sure!" Uncle Sal says, backing away. "Sure! Give everybody my best, then. We're all fine. *Ciao*, Pippino! Sure thing!"

Don Lou gets up from the armchair with difficulty. *Fuck*, he thinks, *maybe I'm the cell that needs eliminating!* His joints are aching so much, he has to lean on Pippino's shoulder.

"I'm going to lie down awhile," he says. "That wine's gone to my head."

TODAY FRANK WAS HORRIFIED TO REALIZE

Today Frank was horrified to realize the whore wasn't acting like a whore anymore, but a wife. Greta was sitting, not on the arm of the armchair, but in the armchair itself, with her legs crossed and her tits thrust forward, sprawling ass flat on the chair, quite relaxed, with a copy of *Cosmopolitan* in her hand and two pins in her hair. Frank remembered that whore Jenny Elemento, a lap dancer that Jack Gravagnuolo married, to everybody's astonishment. "Boys," Jack said to his best friends, "what can I do? Jenny kind of sneaked in and now there she is."

"Get ready, we're going out," Frank said irritably to Greta.

Greta thought, *He's like this because he's in love. All men are grumpy when they're in love. Husbands, for example, are always grumpy! . . . That's why, when it comes to husbands, you have to set limits!* So she said, "I got a headache, Frank."

"What do you mean?" Frank said. "You were so keen to see the Bridge of the Sparrow and now you got a headache!"

"I know, Frank, but it's not my fault if my head is splitting. Why don't you go with Chaz, darling?"

Fuck, the whore called me darling! Frank thought, sitting down on the arm of the chair and stroking her head.

How much fucking lacquer did the bitch put on her hair?

"Your poor little head," Frank said. "Why don't we give it a nice pill, and make that horrible headache go away, eh?"

"Forget about it, Frank. Maybe I'm feeling a bit better already."

Frank jumped away from the whore's chair like he'd been burned.

"All right, then! Let's go see the Sparrow!"

Greta looked at her nails, smoothed her eyebrows with the tip of the middle finger of her right hand, scraped the traces of lipstick from the corners of her mouth, sighed, and said, "Okay, Frank, let's go."

A short bald guy dressed in white, and a tall well-built broad who looks like some kind of nympho whore: one of the paparazzi stationed on Via Crociferi is sure these types who've just appeared at the top of the Alessi steps are who he's waiting for. So he snaps his first pictures, just as Greta is straightening her big tits because the iron whalebone in her bra is pinching her. He's followed by a whole volley of flashes and clicks.

Damn you, Ceccaroli! Frank thinks. *He must have looked in the Catania yellow pages under Weddings!*

Then, for some reason, Frank feels moved. The whole situation: the elegant way he's dressed, the high-class whore by his side, the bodyguard—even Bobby De Niro hasn't got one of those! And he remembers the Sarago, when Carmine Quagliarulo called James Filogamo, the mechanic who had a really good camera, and got him to come over to the restaurant where he, Frank, was manager, and Carmine took photos of the strippers. He said the strippers were crazy about the flashes, it made them feel they were part of the jet set all of a sudden, and when they gave you head after that, they really put their heart and soul into it. Carmine didn't give a fuck about the film. "Forget the photos, the only thing that matters is the flash, to them it's like coming for a guy!" But James put in film all the same, and the next day the whores really busted Carmine's balls because they wanted to see their photos in the paper, so Carmine phoned the publicity department of the New York *Daily News*, where he advertised his chain of laundries, and made arrangements that they'd publish a paragraph. Even he, Frank, appeared in some of those photos, holding a tray of sea bass, or standing waiting while Carmine was busy between some hooker's legs. One time, they even took him to the nightclub and took a photo where he, Frank, was sitting on a little couch, pouring champagne into Carmine's glass, only Carmine was climbing all over Linda, a newcomer from San Giorgio a Cremano, and it looked like Frank was pouring the glass for himself.

And now, Frank thinks, *this is happening to me?*

Trying hard not to be overcome with emotion, Frank does what he used to do when he was a kid, he thinks about something nasty.

What kind of fucking bridge is this Bridge of the Sparrow anyway, it isn't a bridge, just some kind of corridor hung in the air, more like a sewer, you can't even cross it, you just stand under it and think, Great, now I've seen it, what the fuck am I doing here?

"Look at that!" he says to Greta, still smiling at the photographers. "That's where Zeffirelli shot one of the most beautiful scenes in the movie!"

Greta wants to smile happily, and in fact she does smile happily, but it seems to her she's not smiling *completely* happily. Cameron told her once that when you're there, in the middle of things, when you've stopped aimlessly orbiting the world and the world starts revolving radiantly around you, sometimes it get you down and everything seems strange and distant. Even your man, even your parents.

Greta is looking at Frank, who's looking at the bridge that isn't a bridge, and feels there's something wrong. Of course, she's looking at Frank's profile, and in every human being's profile there's always something wrong. Hasn't it ever happened to you to look from close up at the profile of someone you care about? There's always a feeling of strangeness, like, *Is this the profile of the person I love?* Then of course you look at them from the front again and everything goes back to normal.

So Greta glances away from Frank's profile and looks back only when he turns to face her. But damn, there's still something wrong with this picture. Frank's left hand is on his forehead.

Then Greta says the kind of things you say when you don't know what to say: "It's wonderful, Frank!" or "Nice!" or some other crap like that.

Frank puts his hand on her right breast and squeezes it, then clutches her bra, whispers, "Oh, my God!" and kneels, right there in public! Greta thinks, *Oh, my God, what's he doing? Right here, in front of everybody!* Then she hasn't got time to think anything anymore, because she's falling, slowly, dragged down by Frank's fingers clutching the whalebone of her bra. There's something coming out of Frank's forehead, something spurting, like a cuckoo out of a cuckoo clock, but more like a fountain.

Greta wants to go *aaahh* with her mouth, puts her hand on her hair, feels something brush against her nose, turns and sees Chaz, his face completely covered in blood, also falling slowly.

Greta's on the ground now. Just before she faints, she realizes that Chaz has only one eye.

Nuccio laughs, rolling up the car window. The rifle is between his legs, still smoking. Bruno Parrinello is also laughing as he starts the beat-up Mercedes that's been in an accident, and with a squeal of tires drives up the hill toward Via Garibaldi. In less than a minute they're on Piazza di San Cristoforo. Taking a tight bend into a dark, open garage, they scrape the other side of the car (the one that has been intact). The garage door shuts behind them. Nuccio and Bruno get out through one door and they and two other men climb into a dirty white van full of vegetables. The van sets off, its engine sputtering. It stops in front of a parked truck selling hot dogs and french fries. The driver holds out his hand.

The guy in the truck passes him a couple of hot dogs and cans of beer.

DON LOU'S JAGUAR MOVES SILENTLY

Don Lou's Jaguar moves silently along the cobbled streets of the historic center of Catania through crowds of noisy young people. The car turns into a narrow street and all at once the young people disappear. On a corner, set in the stone, a few yards from the ground, a little shrine with a photo and fresh flowers and the words FRANCESCO SPAMPINATO 1967–1985. The name of the neighborhood is San Berillo.

There are many little shrines here, between Via Pistone, Via delle Finanze, and Piazza delle Belle. Showdowns between pimps, there's no escaping it. The windows of the Jaguar are closed, and the air-conditioning and the air freshener keep out the all-pervasive stench of piss. The hookers work in little rooms connecting directly with the street, without running water, and all liquids are thrown out into the street in buckets. Two black girls with big asses, wearing just bras and panties, sway on their heels, leaning forward like they've got backaches. They've got scarred faces: tribal scars or acid, there's no escaping it.

They turn a corner and . . . fuck, look how many there are!

Hookers in every doorway on a street a couple hundred yards long. A Moroccan in a caftan is pushing a supermarket cart loaded with beer and coffee thermoses, a cassette vendor is standing on a corner with watchful eyes and his foot up against the wall.

A black hooker (who must weigh a good two hundred and twenty pounds and has black moles as big as flies all over her face) runs back into her room and shuts herself in, closing the door with a triple lock, safety chains clanging. She must be late with her payments if she's got to lock herself in as soon as a car appears.

The only whore with white skin is sitting in a red nylon slip on a wooden chair reading an out-of-date romance magazine. Next to her dirty feet in a pair of worn slippers is a plastic tray with the remains of a chicken. The hooker is cleaning her teeth with the little finger of her right hand. She watches the Jaguar drive by, with an air of defiance.

Pippino slowly turns left, crosses Via San Giuliano, carries on along Via Casa del Mutilato, and comes out onto Piazza Teatro Massimo, with the opera house on his right. He draws up in front of the Palace of Finance, a monument of fascist architecture in stark contrast to the baroque opera house on the other side of the square.

Pippino quickly gets out of the car, buttons up his jacket, then goes around the car and opens the door for grandfather and grandson. They start walking, Pippino in his brown suit, Don Lou and Lou in dark gray. Pippino walks in front, head bowed.

The door is open. Pippino goes in.

The *picciotti* are sitting around on chairs on the second-floor landing. They're wearing dark suits because it's Sunday, and also because they've been waiting for the *americani*.

For quite a while now, the *picciotti* have been bringing their cards to the landing and playing *briscola*. In the old days there was a constant stream of *picciotti* on mopeds, going back and forth between here and San Berillo, collecting the cash from the hookers' rooms.

But one day Sonnino, after slapping around a hooker who was wearing a Padre Pio medallion between her tits, suddenly smelled the same scent of violets he used to smell in his mother's room, his mother being a woman who was very devoted to the same saint and miraculously escaped death after a serious illness. Since that day, things have changed. His hookers stopped working as hookers. Now they're usherettes in movie theaters, or waitresses in discos and pubs. And all the *picciotti* have to do now is listen to complaints. Dozens of hookers from all over the province come here to complain. They were all planning to put a little something aside so they could buy an apartment in their home village, open a bank account, and find a husband. Now, suddenly, they find themselves in ordinary jobs. Having to deal with the savings and loan. "What the fuck's a savings and loan?" "They ask here for 'place of residence,' what the fuck should I write?"

Not to mention the ones who want a Mercedes.

For the hookers from the villages, this thing with the Mercedes is a real obsession.

"Why the fuck am I turning tricks if I can't drive a Mercedes?" "But you're not turning tricks anymore," the *picciotti* try to explain, "you're a regular worker now." "What the fuck do I care? Everyone in my village knows I'm in the life, and at weekends I show up driving a Panda? Who's going to find me a husband—you?"

Sonnino tried to keep them happy. He'd thought it'd be easy for reformed hookers with steady jobs to find husbands. It turned out that in this city of deadbeats, husbands liked their wives rich, and didn't mind if they were whores.

So, to get them out of the fuckup, Sonnino became a Mercedes dealer. At least it was useful for laundering cash. But in return, they've got to behave like decent women.

And that's the only other job the *picciotti* still have.

If it's discovered the women are trying to turn tricks in the movie theaters, discos, or pubs, they get beaten up, just like in the old days. Even worse, in fact. "Tear 'em to shreds," Sonnino says to his *picciotti*. "Now you've got morality on your side."

The *picciotti* leap to their feet when they see Pippino arrive followed by the *americani*. Bowing and apologizing profusely, they frisk them, then open the door. "Please go in, Signor Sonnino's waiting for you. Please, please, this way."

Sonnino's office is like an upmarket car dealership: lots of chrome, leather armchairs. On the table, a switched-on computer, bills, printed forms, a paperweight in the shape of a model Mercedes.

The walls are covered with photographs. One shows Sonnino, obviously drunk, surrounded by girls in bikinis like Hefner or whatever the fuck's his name. In the photo Sonnino is wearing a loud suit and an orange tie. His right hand is over the shoulder of a topless girl, and there's a piece of metal across four of his fingers, full of blue and red stones that shine in the light from the flash. Lou recognizes it for what it is: brass knuckles, a real collector's item.

In another photo, Sonnino is in his underwear, which is wet and transparent, by the side of a swimming pool. He's holding somebody underwater with his right hand and laughing. With his left hand, he's smoking a cigarette. A man's hand is holding out a drink to him.

Sonnino in the flesh is very different, his face a lot more sunken, its creases set off by his gray stubble. His round red sunglasses seem set into his eye sockets. He sits at his desk with the receiver stuck to his ear, not moving a muscle. He's wearing a black dust coat over a black T-shirt; the dust coat looks like one of those stupid designer items that go for a thousand euros. The desk is too small for someone his height: from beneath it, his frayed jeans are sticking out above silver-studded boots. He looks like a maniac who's occupied a nursery, negotiating the release of the little hostages from a school desk.

The *picciotto* who showed them in dusts down the leather armchairs with a handkerchief before letting the *americani* sit in them. Don Lou and Lou look at each other. Pippino has his usual expression, like everything's completely normal.

"No!" Sonnino says into the receiver. Then he moves it away from his face and gives it a long, puzzled look, like he's never seen anything like it in his life. He slams it down in disgust, crosses his hands on the desk, and regards his guests.

Then he stands up slowly, with difficulty, and bows. "Don Lou, it is an honor for me to meet you. You must forgive me, I was on the phone, and I couldn't let you wait outside. Francesco's making coffee."

"I've heard a lot of good things about you," Don Lou says, looking around.

Sonnino nods. "And this is the famous Pippino the Oleander, right?"

Pippino looks at him like he's already got his death sentence in his pocket.

"*Minchia*, just the way they described him. You know something, Don Lou? When I was still young and handsome, like in these photos, I got sent a gift from Ucciardone, a pit bull puppy that the first thing he did when he was four months old was to bite Maria Annunziata Conception Marletta, a real ballbreaker from Calascibetta, who wanted to leave San Berillo and work the houses along the coast, not realizing her ass was totally fucked. The bitch needed thirty-eight stitches in her calf. And you got to believe this, you know what I called that puppy? I called him Pippino, because the things the Oleander did for you in America were just as famous here in Catania."

Pippino's expression hasn't changed.

"And this," Sonnino continues, indicating Lou, "is your honored grandson. I've heard a lot about him. And I'm really honored that a Hollywood producer trusts me enough to come to my office. I've been hearing a lot of things, and I thought it was really strange that somebody like Lou Sciortino Junior should start work as a *picciotto* for Sal Scali."

"That's precisely why we're here," Don Lou says.

"I know, I know, Don Lou. And I'm at your service. Though I still need to clear this thing up. There's a split-up happening, and all of us are trying to figure out what's going on. What we gotta figure out here is who's still with Virtude, and who's just a fake boss who'd turn his own grandmother. But till the split-up goes down, till they've fucked up, we gotta sit and wait. This is a big organization, and we gotta think about public opinion. These people keep moving the goalposts. Things aren't the way they used to be, it's not black and white anymore. We're with Virtude. We can't stoop to their level. I don't know what the fuck it is, maybe it's the Internet that drives them crazy, maybe it's the modern world, maybe they were born dickheads and we just never noticed before. Oh, yes, I think about all these things, determinism, relativity, social theory, numbers, cardinal numbers, prime numbers, because even mathematics can help Virtude. You ever hear of Hobbes? He was a philosopher. He said, *Homo homini lupus*. In other words, if we can't get along, we cut each other's throats! You see, Don Lou, I think before I act. I also think a lot about Sal Scali, and that asshole Giorgino Favarotta. But they think a lot about me, too. I can kill them, and they can kill me. We have an understanding: I don't bust your balls, you don't bust mine. But now they're going too far. And I don't know how much longer this understanding is going to last. Now I got Don Lou in person here in my office, and I know Sal Scali's been busting your grandson's balls, and I know they're planning a split-up. And I can't find no peace. Peace, you understand me, Don Lou?"

Sonnino looks up and sighs.

"You just keep quiet and let me talk," Tuccio is saying to Nunzio Aliotro. Only Nunzio Aliotro isn't with him. "Where the fuck is he?"

Nunzio Aliotro is standing transfixed by the Jaguar parked in front of the steps of the Palace of Finance on Piazza Teatro Massimo.

"*Minchia*, what an idiot!" Tuccio says, turning back. "What the fuck are you doing?"

"Huh?"

"Will you hurry up?"

"Huh?"

Tuccio looks at Nunzio's reflection in the window of the Jaguar. With his face magnified by the reflection, Nunzio Aliotro looks stupider than ever.

Francesco arrives with the tray of coffee. He places it on the desk, looking curiously at the *americani*. "Sugar?" he asks.

"Don't worry, Francesco. I'll serve the gentlemen."

Francesco bows to Sonnino and the *americani*, and withdraws without turning his back on them.

"Something's gotta give, Don Lou," Sonnino says. "We just need faith. In the meantime, let's have coffee."

On the stairs, Tuccio turns and sees Nunzio standing motionless, looking at the steps.

"What the fuck are you doing?"

"Huh? Climbing the stairs."

"No," Tuccio says, walking back down. "You're not climbing the stairs, you're just looking at them." He mimes the action of climbing the stairs with the index finger and middle finger of his right hand.

"You got to give me time—"

"Time?" Tuccio yanks Nunzio up and makes him go first.

The *picciotti* hear a commotion on the stairs. They look at each other. No, they're not expecting anybody. Artillery emerges from their Sunday suits, like trays of cannoli coming out of the ovens at Caprice on Via Etnea.

Nunzio finds himself staring down the silver-tipped barrel of a full-sized Beretta 96 Steel. From that angle it looks especially big.

"Stop right there!" Tuccio shouts, behind Nunzio's back. "We're here on an errand! We're unarmed! Eh, Francesco, how's your aunt?"

"They've forgotten about Virtude in America, my dear Don Lou," Sonnino says, sipping noisily from his cup. "*Minchia*, Francesco makes some good coffee! That's the reason everything's fucked up. Too much money in circulation, you know, people go crazy. But if you're going to shift the balance in America, you know, you gotta shift it in Sicily, too. Virtude may be in the can, but he's still got papers in his possession that could bring down the U.S. Congress. Those assholes the La Brunas know it, and that twisted little cripple Giorgino Favarotta wants to become head of operations in Sicily. As for that other animal, Sal Scali . . . I don't even want to think about him, Don Lou, or I'll have to take another Prozac, and that'd be my third today! Do you think they go with cholesterol pills? My doctor says no, but I take them anyway! But Don Lou, what can I do right now? They gotta fuck up first. Your grandson, with all due respect, went all over Catania asking questions. Now you arrive, and already they know all about it. People are suspicious, if you ask too many questions, it'll look like you started this whole mess. Did you like the coffee?"

"Excuse me."

"What do you want, Francesco?"

"Tuccio Cramella and Nunzio Aliotro are here. They say Sal Scali sent them."

"Pippino . . ." Don Lou says.

Pippino gets to his feet.

"Send them in. Pippino can stay where he is. They won't recognize you and your grandson from the back."

Pippino looks at Don Lou. Don Lou doesn't nod. If Don Lou nodded, Sonnino would be the first to get his throat cut, followed by Francesco, who wouldn't even have time to react.

"So now let's try to figure out what this is all about," Sonnino says. "Let's bring it out into the open."

"Go in," Francesco says when the *picciotti* have finished frisking them.

Tuccio and Nunzio come into the office with a swagger. "Good evening."

Sonnino doesn't move. Hands folded. Sunglasses as red and round as an Australian sunset.

Which makes Tuccio's smile fade a little. He looks at Pippino, then at the two men who are sitting with their backs to him, motionless.

"We got something to say to you," Tuccio says, looking at the two men like he's saying, *What are you waiting for? Why don't you throw them out?*

Nobody moves.

Tuccio looks at Nunzio with an expression that says, *What are they all, crazy?*

Nunzio isn't moving, either.

Tuccio is getting impatient. "Let's get it over with," he says.

The telephone rings.

Sonnino looks at the telephone. He must have a strange relationship with the telephone, it's obvious from the way he looks at it. He picks up the receiver very slowly, presses it to his ear, and forgets to say hello.

Tuccio looks at Nunzio. Nunzio still isn't moving. Legs wide apart. Hands at his sides. Leather overcoat two sizes too big. He looks up slightly. *Fuck, what a bozo that Nunzio is!*

Don Lou passes a hand over his face.

Lou crosses his legs.

Pippino looks at the photos.

Sonnino is as still as a mummy. He has a strange way of holding the receiver: with his elbow raised.

On the landing, the *picciotti* are dozing. After Sunday lunch, it's nap time.

Sonnino looks at the receiver. Then, as slowly as before, he hangs up. He glances to his right and bends down, looking for something.

Tuccio looks at him.

Sonnino has disappeared.

Strange noises come from behind the desk. Sonnino seems to be unwrapping something. He comes back up again holding a special-issue PA8E military pump-action rifle, with a handle like a pistol.

Tuccio smiles, for some reason, before the shot, fired from a range of six feet, completely blows his face off.

Sonnino looks at the rifle, pleased with himself, and quietly reloads.

The *picciotti* have only just entered the room when they see Nunzio jerk backward five or six feet, as straight and tense as he's always been.

"Peace has arrived, Don Lou. On Via Crociferi they just whacked the *americano*, Frank Erra. We're not taking the blame for this fuck-up. Right now we got to do things like in the old days. Pippino, don't feel so bad. I'm not as quick as you are, I gotta rely on the element of surprise, that's why I use these fucking rifles even though they keep making them more and more complicated. I pull out a .22, I wouldn't have time to explain, you'd have cut my head off already with a knife. Which would have been wrong. Because I respect Don Lou as much as you do."

The *picciotti* who've come running into the room don't know what the fuck to do.

"Clean this up, okay? They wanted a split-up, we'll give them one. They try busting Sonnino's balls, this is what happens!" He stands up. "Please, Don Lou, after you."

UNCLE SAL AND DON GIORGINO ARE SITTING IN THE BACKSEAT OF THE MERCEDES

ncle Sal and Don Giorgino are sitting in the backseat of the Mercedes, parked on what is officially Piazza Vittorio Emmanuele, but because it's on Via Umberto everybody calls it Piazza Umberto.

The *picciotto* who's working as Don Giorgino's driver is standing on the sidewalk in front of Palazzo Cappellani, smoking a cigarette and watching the women go by.

Don Giorgino has suddenly fallen silent in the middle of talking. Uncle Sal looks at him, and can't tell if he's asleep or not.

Don Giorgino sometimes does this: dozes off in the middle of saying something. Uncle Sal doesn't know what to do because Don Giorgino always wears sunglasses and you can never be sure if he's asleep or just thinking.

Then Don Giorgino, leaning on his walking stick, starts falling to his left. Uncle Sal moves closer to the door, because it doesn't seem right for Don Giorgino to doze off on his shoulder. Anybody passing sees that, God knows what they're gonna think.

When Don Giorgino sent for Uncle Sal, he made it clear he wanted to see him immediately. And when Uncle Sal heard that Don Giorgino wanted to see him *in the car*, he wasted no time in getting to Piazza Umberto because you get summoned to meet *in a car* only when something really serious has happened, something that's got to be dealt with quickly and you're afraid of being bugged.

"But in your opinion . . ." Don Giorgino says, jerking awake, "in your opinion, does she like sperm?"

Don Giorgino bursts into a laugh that almost makes Uncle Sal jump. Then he looks at Uncle Sal, very serious all of a sudden. Uncle Sal is tense and alert now. Don Giorgino starts laughing again.

Uncle Sal half smiles, not understanding a fucking thing.

"Sperm . . ." Don Giorgino says, coughing now instead of laughing, "Spunk!" and clears his throat.

Uncle Sal still doesn't know what the fuck he's talking about. *What has sperm got to do with anything?*

"Well . . . yes, I guess so . . ." he says, to be on the safe side.

Don Giorgino stops clearing his throat and looks at him very seriously. It's obvious he's very serious because, even though he's wearing sunglasses and you can't see his eyes, his mouth is just a thin line and a thread of foam is slithering down his chin.

Did I say something wrong? Uncle Sal thinks.

This time Don Giorgino laughs in a way where you can't tell if he's laughing, crying, shouting, swearing, or dying. There's a bit of everything—coughing, clearing his throat, swaying, spitting, sucking, whistling—before it stops abruptly.

Fuck! Uncle Sal thinks.

Don Giorgino opens the door and spits on the sidewalk.

"That's what I'm telling you," he says, his voice clear at last. "The whore's still alive."

"Who?"

"What do you mean, who? What the fuck's she called? The one with the German name! You said just now, the one who likes sperm . . ."

"Who? Greta? Frank Erra's whore?"

"Nuccio's a dickhead who should thank that good woman his mother he's still alive . . . Did I ever tell you his mother came to us when we went to the mattresses and blew us all?"

"Yes, of course you told me, Don Giorgino. But what are you telling me, the whore's still alive? That's impossible!"

"You want me to slap you around or what? I'm telling you, she's alive, alive!" Don Giorgino raises both hands, palms upturned toward heaven.

"Wait till I get my hands on Nuccio . . ." Uncle Sal says, his face turning red. "Wait till I get my hands on him . . ."

"Calm down or you'll have a heart attack . . ." Don Giorgino says. "You don't have to get your hands on him, because whores are like that, they never die, they're worse than cockroaches! She wasn't even hit, just grazed. She got a hole in her hair!"

"A hole in her hair?"

"Yes, they tell me she got a kind of . . ." Don Giorgino mimes a kind of hole through the woman's hairdo. "Anyhow, they didn't get her . . ."

"And where is she now?"

"They're taking her to the Central Palace."

"The Central Palace?"

"My *picciotto* at Garibaldi Hospital told me the doctors said she had to be kept under observation for twenty-four hours because she banged her head. When they told her they didn't have a bed and she'd have to sleep on a gurney in the corridor, she started screaming . . . So they gave her Valium . . . they say she was having hysterics . . . so to get rid of her they brought her the register, made her sign, and told her to fuck off. Then the cops said they had to take her to police headquarters and interrogate her. But then the examining magistrate came to police headquarters, and the anti-Mafia squad, and the press and TV and every son of a bitch in the country, and she started screaming again. They gave her another dose of Valium and told her to fuck off from there, too. They told her if she stopped screaming they'd go with her to the hotel and then they'd see."

"*Minchia*, Don Giorgino, I'll send for Nuccio right away."

"Shut up and don't do anything else stupid. Phone Turi."

Uncle Sal looks at him in terror. "Turi?"

"I said phone Turi."

Uncle Sal feels a strong desire to cross himself. Maybe not so much, but Uncle Sal does have nieces, so he'd prefer not to have anything to do with Turi.

"What are you waiting for?"

"Okay, I'll do it now . . ."

Don Giorgino nods.

Uncle Sal takes the cell phone and, cursing with his eyes, dials Turi's number.

"But couldn't Nuccio take care— Turi?" Uncle Sal says, his voice shaking like a tulip ruffled by the wind.

"Yes?" a voice hisses.

Uncle Sal nods to Don Giorgino.

It's not clear if Don Giorgino is sleeping.

"This is Sal Scali . . ."

"Good evening . . ."

Making an effort, Uncle Sal says, "Listen, Turi, I need you to do something for me . . ."

"Yes?"

"Right now, at the Central Palace. An *americana* who arrived from Rome with a guy named Frank Erra . . ."

"Do you want me to do him, too?"

"No, he already got whacked . . . The woman's name is Greta, I don't know her last name . . ."

"I'm at your disposal, Don Sal . . ."

Uncle Sal hears a kind of sucking sound and is about to hang up when Don Giorgino says, "Pass me the phone."

Uncle Sal takes the cell phone and gives it to Don Giorgino.

Don Giorgino looks right and left, takes the phone, and says in a low voice, "It's me. Did you get the things?"

Then Don Giorgino hangs up, passes the phone to Uncle Sal, leans on his cane again, and starts laughing, fuck him, this time making even the *picciotto* who got out of the car turn around, just as he was looking at a woman who, if she ever got hold of your dick, you'd have to send the marshal to her house to get it back.

THE TELEPHONE RINGS
IN TONY'S HOUSE

The telephone rings in Tony's house.

"It can explode for all I care, I'm not answering," Cettina says.

Cettina is feeling pretty nervous right now, because the day started with Tony showing up with a six-pack of beer in his hand and asking, "Did you iron my shirts?"

Tony has this thing that his shirts have to be ironed by his wife because if they're ironed by the maid it's obvious they haven't been ironed with love.

"Yes, Tony, they're upstairs in the basket with the ironing."

"All of them?"

When there's a barbecue, Tony wears Indian silk shirts, which he has to change every fifteen minutes, because they get rings of sweat under his armpits.

"Yes, Tony, every single one."

"I hope you didn't starch them."

"No, I didn't starch them, Tony."

"Because," Tony said to the girls, who'd come to lend a hand to get ready for the barbecue, "the collar of an Indian silk shirt has gotta be soft."

"I made them soft for you, Tony."

Tony first made a face like he was saying, *Good*, then his expression changed abruptly and he asked, "Why aren't these beers in the fridge?"

Cettina looked at the beers.

"Because they wouldn't fit, Tony. The fridge is full of beer."

"Always ready with an excuse, aren't you? What do you mean, they don't fit? I told you a thousand times, you gotta lay beers flat in the fridge." With his hands Tony mimed beers lying flat. "That way they go in better."

"I put them in flat."

"How flat?"

"Tony, I couldn't find mayonnaise in the kitchen," Valentina said.

Tony put a hand on his head, like he was trying to keep it from spinning, and ran into the kitchen.

Cettina thanked Valentina for getting Tony out of her hair. And at that moment the phone rang.

"It can explode for all I care, I'm not answering," Cettina says.

"Maybe it's the *americano* from last time," Cinzia says.

Cettina grimaces, thinking about the double dose of matchmaking Tony's planning.

"What *americano*?" Mindy says.

"The one you were eating alive," Alessia says.

"I wasn't eating anyone alive," Mindy says, her face lighting up.

"Is it true she was looking at him?" Cinzia asks Aunt Carmela.

"If she says she wasn't looking at him, she wasn't looking at him," Aunt Carmela says.

"*Minchia*," Rosy says, "if Steve sees something like that, he slaps me around, he's so jealous. I don't get it with Steve, first he wants me to dress feminine, then he slaps me because they look."

"Yes, Rosy, but you dress too feminine!" Valentina says.

"And you dress like a man!"

There's a noise of broken bottles coming from the kitchen.

"I told you they wouldn't fit," Cettina says, looking into space.

"Fuck, I nearly cut myself," Tony says, coming back from the kitchen. Then he stops, listens, looks at the women lying around, and asks, "Sorry to bother you, but point of information: don't any of you hear the phone?"

"We all thought you wanted to answer it," Valentina says. "You always get pissed off that we don't know how to answer the phone."

"Of course I get pissed off. Cettina says hello like she's gonna bite off somebody's hand."

Tony picks up the receiver and says, "Yes?" Then he turns white and hangs up silently. He's facing the women, but it's like he isn't looking at anybody.

The girls and Aunt Carmela look at each other.

"Fuck . . ." Tony says.

"Fuck what?" Cettina says, shifting the centerpiece on the table, then moving it back where it was before.

"Fuck . . . it was the *americano* . . ."

"The *americano*?" Mindy says, getting up.

"He told me he's bringing Leonard Trent . . . A celebrity, in my house. I can't get my head around it!"

SCIACCA AND LONGO
NEVER CATCH A BREAK

Sciacca and Longo never catch a break. The brass on Via Vecchia Ognina always give them the dirtiest jobs, stakeouts, escorts, an endless regimen of shit, with no consideration for length of service and merit.

Sciacca and Longo were drinking an *amaro* at Caprice—they needed a *digestivo* after Sciacca's sister's eggplant pasta and Longo's wife's pasta with sardines—when Via Vecchia Ognina ordered them to pick up the American woman who was having hysterics and escort her back to her hotel.

Obviously, Sciacca and Longo were overjoyed at having to give up their *amaro* to play escort to an American in hysterics.

In the elevator, they're almost falling asleep when Greta starts screaming, calling Longo a *bastard* and Sciacca a *son of a bitch*.

It's normal, Longo thinks. *They just whacked her pimp, and it's a well-known fact that hookers always act this way when their pimps get whacked.*

When they reach her floor, Sciacca takes Greta's arm, and the hooker starts screaming, "Don't touch me!"

But Sciacca and Longo still take her as far as her room. Greta looks at them and slams the door in their faces.

On the landing, Longo takes out a little bottle of *sambuca* he filched from the cash desk at the Caprice, and they're blissfully knocking it back when an asshole in a blue jacket and gray pants, with dandruff on his lapels, shows up.

"Good evening," he says.

Longo and Sciacca look at each other and nod in reply.

The asshole has red hair and a very taut face like somebody who's had plastic surgery. Only this one looks here and there like he's had it one too many times. His face has been lifted so much, his eyes are like little almonds.

"What's going on? First I hear a woman screaming, now there's two cops in the corridor. Nothing to worry about, I hope?"

"Nothing, nothing, just a murder," Longo says. "The lady was involved. She's still in shock."

"A murder here? In the hotel?"

"No, outside."

"Nothing serious, I hope . . ." the guy says, referring to the murder. "But this lady, was she really involved or did she just happen to be there?"

Longo and Sciacca look at each other again.

"Just keep moving," Sciacca says, waving the hand that's holding the *sambuca*.

"Okay, okay. I was thinking about you guys. If the lady just happened to be there, well, these things happen. But if she's actually involved and she got away, I mean, they're likely to try again, aren't they? *Salutiamo.*"

The guy with the blue jacket and gray pants puts his hands in his pockets and walks away.

"What an asshole," Sciacca says.

"Face-lift Charlie," Longo says.

Sciacca and Longo start laughing. Sciacca passes the *sambuca* to Longo, and Longo knocks it back.

"What did the boss tell you?" Sciacca asks.

"*Minchia*, Licciardello was wound up like a violin string! The FBI's been in touch with him, seems one of the two dead guys on Via Crociferi is a big capo!"

"And we gotta stay here?" Sciacca says, putting his hands in his pockets and hunching his shoulders.

"Starting to feel cold, huh? Fucking air-conditioning!" Longo says.

"Fuck, it's like a cold wind came in! Listen, Longo! Did Licciardello say, 'Take her to the hotel and keep an eye on her' or 'Take her to the hotel and keep an eye on the hotel'?"

"The second one, I think," Longo says, laughing.

"So we could go down to the bar and get another Fernet?"

"I'd say definitely yes," Longo says.

On the stairs, Sciacca and Longo pass the asshole with a face like a Chinaman, on his way back up the stairs.

As usual, Turi's got a tape recorder in his pocket. He likes to play back the victim's whimpers later. Greta comes out of the shower and Turi grabs her by the shoulders, puts his hand over her mouth, lays her out on the bed, and puts the knife to her throat. Turi can feel the whore starting to panic, her heart going boom-boom-boom, her breath coming in little gasps. Then she starts writhing on the bed. Whenever he presses the blade in, the whore screams, when he presses less, she relaxes, when he presses it in again, she tenses again.

Then the whore calms down, like she's trying to make it easier for him. Turi has seen a lot of things in his life, but never a whore with a knife at her throat starting to open and close her ass.

This sends Turi practically into a swoon. The masochistic whore is writhing at a faster rhythm now and Turi is getting aroused, especially as his dick is rubbing against the zipper of his pants.

The only part of Greta's body that's free is her arm, which is dangling over the side of the bed. With the tips of her fingers, she feels the carpet, searching for something, anything, a hair grip, a hatpin. And all she can find are the Prada shoes with stiletto heels that Chaz, on Frank's orders, bought her on Fifth Avenue.

When the edge of the heel hits him on the nose, Turi feels uncomfortable at first. Everything turns white, and then, suddenly, he can feel his nose getting bigger. And he remembers an afternoon when he was still a kid and he suddenly felt his pecker itching and getting bigger and he went into the john to play with it and it was just like when you squeezed your zits and this very white stuff like a kind of pus came out of his hard dick. Turi relaxes, with an almost ecstatic expression on his face.

Greta gathers all her strength, grips the stiletto heel in her right hand, and drives it hard into his eye, then she kneads the heel in with both hands, the way she used to watch her grandmother knead bread on those long Maine afternoons. She hears a noise, not even a noise, a whisper, something like a sigh of pleasure coming out of Turi's mouth. After that, nothing. Only then does Greta look her assailant in the face. And she sees her thousand-dollar shoe embedded in the guy's eye. He's lying still and silent now. From the base of the shoe, a thick blotch of blood starts spreading over a face that's had more lifts than Cher.

TO FIND A NERO D'AVOLA

To find a Nero d'Avola the way Don Lou wanted it ("Don't just buy the first one you find, and not from oak casks, please"), Pippino had to go around half of Catania, because at the Central Palace and around the hotel they had Nero d'Avola, but bottled in Venice, which, Don Lou told Lou, was like buying Murano glass made in Carrapipi. Now, sitting in his armchair in his suite at the Palace, Don Lou is sipping it slowly. "*Minchia*, this is a wine!"

Sitting in another armchair, behind Don Lou, Pippino nods contentedly. He's just started reading a book he heard a lot about in America, and he likes the beginning: *In my younger and more vulnerable years my father gave me some advice . . .* Fuck, his father used to do the same when he was a kid!

"I drank a really good white wine from oak casks, Grandpa," Lou says, his voice slurred by gin and cigarettes.

Sciortino Junior is sitting on the couch facing Don Lou's armchair, knocking back his third gin and tonic of the day.

"I'm not saying wine from casks isn't good," Don Lou says, "I'm saying it's a French thing, and the cask affects the taste." Then, irritably, maybe because his hemorrhoids are bothering him, "But what the fuck are you still doing here? I told you I want people to see you around!"

"Don't worry, Grandpa!" Lou says. "I've been invited to a barbecue by Sal Scali's nephew Tony, with that dickhead Leonard Trent! I'll show up in a red jacket. They'll see me, all right!"

"A barbecue?" Don Lou says. "A barbecue in Catania? Maybe they said a buffet!"

"Barbecue, they said barbecue."

"So this Tony's an idiot," Don Lou says. "Better still!" Then, looking toward the window that gives onto Via Etnea, "What's that noise? What is that, a fire truck or the cops?"

"Let me go see," Pippino says, putting the book down on the carpet. Don Lou nods. Pippino looks around, sees the bottle of gin, puts it back in the minibar—watched by a not very happy Lou—and leaves the room.

"*Minchia*," Don Lou says, "everything's changed in Sicily! Even the sirens!"

Lou nods, even though he hasn't got a fucking clue what the sirens used to sound like.

Don Lou grips the glass of Nero d'Avola with his right hand and the arm of the chair with his left, and starts tapping the left foot of the chair repeatedly with his right foot.

"I can't get my head around what Sonnino told us!" he says. "Draw your own conclusions. Sergeants getting their heads blown off, *americani* fucking with us and getting killed on Via Crociferi—because it's obvious it was them, a famous producer in full view of a bunch of photographers—a boss has got to ask himself, is that how Virtude controls his territory? *Capish*, Lou? Here they've been using us to fuck Virtude, and in America they want Sicily to fuck us up the ass!" Don Lou slams his fist down on the left arm of the chair.

"And Sal Scali?" he continues. "*Minchia*, he used to be the biggest ass kisser, now look at him feeling his oats! When those dickhead *picciotti* of his dropped the sergeant, the asshole thought he'd put you in the middle. So the whole of Catania started to ask, *Who the fuck is this Lou Sciortino? What the fuck does he want with us?* But, *minchia*, now we're going to fucking show him!"

Don Lou slams his fist down so hard on the arm of the chair that the wine spills on his white shirt, near his heart.

When Pippino comes back in the room and sees the red stain on his heart, he looks so horrified that Don Lou quickly says, "It's Nero d'Avola."

Pippino coughs and says, "Mr. Trent wants to talk to you. I met him down in the lobby. He knows what's going on, I'm sure of it."

"Where is he now?" Don Lou asks.

"Waiting outside."

"So show him in!"

Leonard comes in quickly while Lou is trying to clean the stain from Don Lou's shirt with a wet towel.

"Oh, Lord," he says, stopping abruptly. "The killer was here, too!"

"It's Nero d'Avola," Don Lou says irritably. "Now, what's this about the killer?"

"Jesus Christ, didn't you hear? The hotel's turned upside down, ambulances, police, prosecutors!" Leonard sits down on the couch, sighs, and crosses his legs. "Can I have a little of that wine, Pippino?" he asks. "Fuck, I lost my producer—almost lost my producer's lover!"

"Who?" Don Lou says. "Frank Erra's whore? Didn't they whack her on Via Crociferi?"

"All they did was ruin her hairdo under the Bridge of the Sparrow, Don Lou! The bacons spent half a day interrogating her, then sent her under escort to this fucking hotel. An escort like that, who needs enemies, as my father would have said. The killer walked right up to her room, opened the door, and attacked her in the shower!"

"*Minchia*, they whacked her here, practically next door?" Don Lou says, slamming his fist down again on the arm of the chair.

"Thanks, Pippino," Leonard says, grabbing the glass of Nero d'Avola. "No, she's not dead, Don Lou, the killer's dead."

"What do you mean, the killer's dead?"

"Stone dead, with a Prada stiletto heel hammered into his left eye. Now Greta's screaming to the bacons and the prosecutors that she wants her shoe back. She says it's worth more than a thousand dollars!"

"Fuck," Lou says, raising the glass of gin in a toast, "you should use that scene in your next movie, Leonard, it's perfect!"

"Why couldn't you turn out normal?" Don Lou snaps, his face turning red. "The Gabellas, the Gaglianos, the Cultreras, they all got normal grandsons! *Minchia*, a situation like this, you think it's funny?!"

"If you want me to, Grandpa, I'll do what Jack Gagliano did!" Lou says resentfully.

Don Lou emits an incomprehensible whine.

"What did Jack Gagliano do?" Leonard asks.

"To get at Anthony Fumeri," Lou says, "he grabbed Anthony's brother, cut his hand off, put the rest of the body in formaldehyde, and sent the hand all wrapped up and packed in ice so it didn't stink, with a card that read, *We've given you one hand, now we request a meeting. If you refuse to grace us with your presence, we'll take no offense, but as the good Christians we are, we'll turn the other cheek, and send you the other hand.* I could do that to Sal Scali. Maybe I could kidnap Tony."

"Who's Tony? The guy throwing the party?" Leonard asks.

"Right, the guy throwing the barbecue, Sal Scali's nephew," Lou says.

"Don't do a fucking thing!" Don Lou says very seriously. "I want you to be a good kid. Show Leonard around Catania. Go to barbecues with these bozos, go to their fucking parties, see Via Etnea, see the whole of Catania, the whole of Sicily, damn it! And I want everybody to see you while you're doing it. Do we understand each other?"

Lou and Leonard look at each other, puzzled.

"In fact, why don't you start right now?" Don Lou says, looking even more severe.

Lou nods to his grandpa and signals to Leonard that it's time for a change of scene. Reluctantly, Leonard puts the glass of Nero d'Avola down on the coffee table, stands up, and shakes his leg to straighten the crease in his pants.

"'Bye, Don Lou," he says.

Don Lou raises his left hand slightly.

Alone with Don Lou, Pippino does what he's careful to avoid doing in public: he takes a blanket and arranges it tenderly over Don Lou's legs. Don Lou, as usual, pretends not to like it, and shifts the blanket to one side, mumbling, "*Minchia*, barbecues in Catania! Maybe the assholes play baseball, too!" Then he adds plaintively, "I can't get up! Get the good cell phone, Pippino, and call John La Bruna for me."

Pippino smiles, tucks in the blanket on the side that's uncovered, goes to the wardrobe, takes a cell phone out of a bag, dials John La Bruna's number, says, "Wait a minute," and passes the device to Don Lou.

"Ciao, John," Don Lou says. "This is Lou Sciortino."

"Where are you calling from, Lou?" At the other end of the line, John La Bruna's voice doesn't sound too happy.

"Don't worry, John, the line's safe."

"Where are you?"

"In Sicily, John. I wanted to tell you, that thing you sent me at Starship less than a month ago, it got damaged."

Pippino sits down on the edge of the couch, ready to spring up again.

"Don't worry, Lou, we can send you a replacement. You know, we La Brunas always give a guarantee with our merchandise."

"Listen, John, the truth is, I'm tired, I'm old, I got arteriosclerosis, and my grandson is a reliable person. You know what I'm saying? The movie business isn't for me anymore."

John La Bruna is silent for five or six seconds. Then he says, "I understand, Lou! We're getting old for such things . . ."

"Exactly. Listen, John, here's the deal, I go back to New York, bring my grandson back with me, we draw up a nice contract, in black and white, saying I sell you Starship . . ."

"But are you sure I want to buy it, Lou? *Cazzarola*, I got so much tax to pay right now!"

"John . . . how about you name a price, okay? And if you haven't got the cash, don't worry, I won't sue."

John laughs uproariously. "Sure, Lou, sure . . . So what are you going to do, retire?"

"More or less, John, more or less."

"I understand. You want to devote yourself to opera. What are you doing, taking singing lessons? You want to be like Salvatore Mineo, who performed under the dome of Montreal Cathedral? But what's with us Italians and opera? I say we should get it out of our systems, Lou! There's only one Pavarotti, damn it, the others all sing off-key."

"No, John, when I want to sing, I sing!" Don Lou says. "I can't help it, opera's my passion. If they don't want me to sing, they'll have to kill me . . . Not that I'm recommending it to anybody else . . ."

"Of course, Lou, of course. But don't you have any other passions?"

"I could devote myself to agriculture."

"Why don't you?"

"Because lately, I started planting beans, and they came out small, sad, and bitter . . . Then I tried almonds . . . But you know what happened? They dried up! The almonds dried up! I need to eliminate the few broken beans I still got left, the almonds, too . . . What do you think, John?"

"Great idea, Lou. Eliminate, eliminate, it's the only way to renew the soil!"

"Are you sure, John?"

"*Cazzarola*, Lou. I've never liked beans or almonds. It's an obsession you Sicilians have. I assure you, Lou, as far as I'm concerned, they could get rid of all the beans and almonds in the world! Who gives a shit, right?"

"How's Carmine Iacono, John? And Salvatore Fumeri? Tell them they're assholes, because they don't work with Don Lou Sciortino anymore!"

"They're fine, Lou. They always remember you with affection."

"Okay, John, it was a pleasure talking to you."

"Likewise, Lou. So, I'll expect you in New York . . . In the meantime, I'll get Charlie Cacace to draw up a contract, he's a good kid and—"

"You do whatever you think is right, John."

"Okay, Lou, 'bye."

"'Bye, John."

Don Lou throws the cell phone on the coffee table, picks up the glass of Nero d'Avola, but doesn't drink it. He stays like that, with the blanket over his knees, bent forward slightly, looking into the glass. Then he looks up slightly and meets Pippino's eyes. Pippino is tense. Don Lou lowers his head again, then nods. Pippino jumps to his feet and straightens his pants.

THE ROOM IS DIMLY LIT

The room is dimly lit by a kerosene lamp, the kind used in camping. A leather jacket is hanging on the back of a bottomless chair, and a cell phone is ringing inside the pocket. Underneath the sound of the phone, the squeak of bedsprings can briefly be heard.

"What the fuck!" Nuccio says. He gets up, naked, and goes to get the cell phone. "What the f— Don Scali!"

"Where the fuck are you?"

"We had a flat. Parrinello's changing the tire on the van."

"So to kill time, you go to whores . . ."

"No, Don Scali, don't say these things . . ."

"*Minchia*, what is it with you? Every time you whack somebody, you got to get laid afterwards?"

"No, Don Scali, who told you that? . . . I'm in a . . . in a bar."

"Sure you are. You whack somebody, you eat a hot dog, you take a tab of ecstasy, and you get laid, and then you show up smelling of some black whore. You think I don't know you? If you're not here, if you're not here *right now*, I'll cut off your balls and wear them for earrings . . . *capish?* . . . I'll wear them for fucking earrings!"

"I'll be there, Don Scali, *minchia*, even if the wheel is broken, I don't care, I'll tell Bruno to leave it, I'll finish my Fernet and I'll be there . . . No, no, I won't even finish it . . . I'll be right there . . ."

It's dusk in the Simeto estuary, and the sun is setting over the reeds and the birds, over bags of garbage, a few squatters' shacks, old shoes, sewage from the drains, and also over the corpses of Tuccio and Nunzio Aliotro. Tuccio is lying facedown, Nunzio is in a contorted position with his right arm tensed. From a hundred yards, they look like a contemporary art installation. Tuccio's cell phone rings: the ringtone is "La Vida Loca. "

With a wrapped-up package under his arm, Nuccio looks right and left along Corso Italia and rings at the door of Scali's Amaretti. *Maria*, he really loves plotting something after a good fuck with a black girl in San Berillo!

Uncle Sal opens the brass and glass door, looks at Nuccio, and gives him a slap that echoes along Corso Italia.

"Did you think this was the right moment to get laid?"

"Don Scali, I swear to you, I went and had a Fernet . . ."

"Did you bring the rifle?"

"Sure, here it is . . ." Nuccio says, lifting the package. "I wrapped it so nobody would see it . . ."

"Where's Tuccio?"

"Are you asking me, Don Scali? He went to take care of Sonnino, didn't he?"

"Didn't you talk on your cell?"

"No."

"You phone each other when you're sitting in the same car, and today you didn't talk on the phone?"

"Okay, we sometimes do that as a joke, but we don't joke when we're working."

"You stupid bastard, you motherfucking, cocksucking son of a bitch!"

Maybe it's because he's high, or maybe it's because he's used to it, but here in Sciortino Junior's office, Nuccio just smiles when Uncle Sal calls him names. And that makes Uncle Sal even angrier.

"You son of a fucking bitch. Don't you know your mother gave us all head when we went to the mattresses? I had to call Turi to get rid of that fucking *americana* whore! *Capish*, you big faggot?"

"That's not possible, Don Scali, I saw the *americano* in the white suit go down, and she went down at the same time!"

"The bitch went down, did she, you cocksucking faggot? You're laughing? You faggots are all the same, you love to laugh!"

"I'm not laughing, Don Scali, I'm not laughing," Nuccio says, laughing.

"Hide the rifle down there!" Uncle Sal says, pointing to Lou's wardrobe.

Nuccio pulls his pants up, takes the rifle, gets down on his knees, puts his head right inside the wardrobe, and starts rummaging around.

"Did you put your gloves on, dickhead?"

"Of course!" Nuccio says, thinking of the black girl slipping the condom on his dick.

"Be careful, if the thing goes off, it'll blow your faggot face off."

"What?" Nuccio asks from the back of the wardrobe.

"I said be careful, if it goes off, it'll blow your faggot face off."

"What did you say, Don Scali?"

"Go fuck yourself, I said go fuck yourself."

Nuccio comes out of the wardrobe with his eyes half closed, gets to his feet, and wipes the dust off his knees. "What do we do now?" he asks.

Uncle Sal is staring into space. Nuccio makes a dumb face. He looks around and sees a bottle of gin. He looks at Uncle Sal. But Uncle Sal is absorbed by something that's going on in his head. Nuccio moves the bottle closer, glances at Uncle Sal out of the corner of his eye, unscrews the top, takes a glass, pours the gin, glances at Uncle Sal again, knocks back the gin, puts down the glass, puts his hands in his pockets, and whistles.

"Call Tuccio," Uncle Sal says, still staring into space. Then he gets up on tiptoe and falls back on his heels.

Nuccio takes the phone and dials Tuccio's number.

In the Simeto estuary are couples fucking in their cars, plastic bags, sand dunes with plastic bottles half buried in them, the corpses of Tuccio and Nunzio, and "La Vida Loca" playing on a cell phone.

"Answer it, it must be your wife," somebody says from one of the cars.

They all laugh. Then they go back to fucking.

"No answer," Nuccio says, not knowing what the fuck to do, rummaging through the documents and newspapers and overturned beer bottles on the desk. Then suddenly he sees the crossbow.

"Give me the phone!" Uncle Sal says.

Nuccio gives Uncle Sal the cell and starts walking around the room. He takes the bottle of gin from the bar, unscrews the top, and pours himself another glass. When the glass is full, he starts walking around the room again, then sits back down on a chair at the desk, absently. He looks into space and feels like laughing.

"What the fuck are you doing?"

"Eh?"

"What the fuck are you laughing about?"

"Who, me? I'm not laughing, Don Scali," Nuccio says, taking a swig of the gin.

Uncle Sal lets it pass. He dials a number.

Nuccio puts his elbow on the desk, but so close to the edge that it slips off. Then he opens the top right-hand drawer of the desk and sees the box of arrows for the crossbow.

Nuccio looks at it out of the corner of his eye. It looks like one of those old cookie boxes, but it has the word ARROWS on it. Nuccio takes it out, puts it on the desk, and opens it.

"Nunzio Aliotro's got music playing," Uncle Sal says.

Nuccio takes out an arrow and starts stroking the goose quills. "Huh?" he says.

"Music, on the phone," Uncle Sal says.

Nuccio brings the tip of the arrow up close to his right eye, then blinks, moves the arrow farther away, puts it down next to the crossbow, and at last his thoughts come into focus. He smiles as he pulls on the string and turns the steel knob that holds back the string and the arrow.

"Where the fuck are you? This is Sal Scali!" Uncle Sal says into the phone, then gets up on tiptoe and, just as he's about to fall back on his heels, finds himself incomprehensibly, mysteriously, on the ground. Just before he stops seeing any fucking thing at all, Uncle Sal has time to see a bloodstain descending rapidly, from right to left, over his white shirt, obliterating the beautifully embroidered gothic SS on the left side of the shirt.

TONY PHONED THE CHINESE
RESTAURANT ON VIA PACINI

Tony phoned the Chinese restaurant on Via Pacini. The bozo who answered didn't understand a fucking thing, then someone with more upstairs came on the phone and now, at the barbecue, along with the shooting stars, the colored balloons, the lanterns, some lighted and some of them not, there's a dragon about thirty feet long winding its way across the garden.

Tony's last big barbecue of the season is in honor of Senator Zappulla, who helped Tony get his hairdresser's license. Tony has invited people with money, from every milieu (that's the word he used to Cettina), so Senator Zappulla can come and give everybody a smile and a promise, because he knows it takes a lot of bricks to build a wall.

But because there are *americani* here, too, this time, Tony thought of something special, an evening of *chinoiserie et orientalisme*—those are the very words he used to Cettina—with a triad of aperitifs, Bellini, Rossini, and Tonini—prosecco, licorice, and coconut milk, white and black just like the cardinal, who for some reason Tony is convinced is Sicilian-American—Sicilian sushi, anchovies and raw octopus, and at the octopus buffet, of course, Nunzio and

Agatino dressed as Yakuza: tight-fitting black leather jeans, patent leather moccasins with square tips and big silver buckles, tight vests, leather jackets, opaque sunglasses.

Looking contentedly at the dragon, Tony stops Nunzio as he passes and asks in a low voice, "Are there enough amaretti?"

Nunzio, who's short, looks him up and down. "If there aren't, you can always get more from Corso Italia," he says irritably.

"Then hurry up and find some, asshole!" Tony says, reflected in Nunzio's sunglasses. Then he realizes that from that angle, his reflection looks twice the size, and he gives himself a manual face-lift, smoothing his neck several times very quickly with his hand to dismiss even the memory of skin that's starting to age.

Felice Romano, the mechanic, and Angelo Colombo, the dressmaker, are talking in a corner of the garden. Felice is wearing a caftan with Indian pants, Angelo a white linen suit like the one Truman Capote wore when he visited Taormina. They're talking but not really, because Felice doesn't give a shit what Angelo's saying, and vice versa. What they're really doing is vamping, and watching everyone else do the same.

Angelo's wife, who used to model for him before they were married, leans over to Felice's wife, who's wearing a blue medium-length skirt, white tights, and a blouse with an embroidered collar, and whispers in her ear, "Since he stopped fucking me, all he does is talk. Same with you?"

"Tell me about it, signora. Sometimes I really worry."

"I'm telling you," Uncle Mimmo is saying a few yards away, buttoning his woolen jacket over his checkered shirt, "you got to explain this democracy to me."

Cosimo, Pietro, Turi, and Tano nod. They've been invited to a political barbecue, so it's normal to talk politics, like when you go to the theater it's normal to talk about Pirandello.

"*Minchia*, at least when there was a king, you knew who you had to shoot. The way things are now, who understands a fucking thing? You're telling me," he continues, turning to Cosimo, even though Cosimo hasn't said a fucking thing, "in a democracy, the guy behaves badly, you stop voting for him." Uncle Mimmo gives a bitter laugh. "But the guy doesn't give a shit, all he does is change sides, and you can't even shoot him because that's democracy."

Cosimo nods.

"*Minchia*, in a democracy politicians run faster than rabbits."

Signorina Niscemi has brought Raffaella, her best friend, who's a cleaning woman at the provincial assembly.

"Are you sure it was okay for me to come?" Raffaella asks, a tad embarrassed. "I wasn't invited."

"Sure! You can bring anybody you like to a political barbecue. In fact, the more people you bring, the better."

Signorina Niscemi isn't wearing a bra, and the daisies on her blouse look like they're being shaken by a tornado in California or Florida—someplace in America with palms.

Raffaella, on the other hand, is wearing a tight bra, which lifts her tits and makes them sway, so she's looking good, too.

"Okay, but I feel embarrassed all the same. I don't know anybody."

"Just do what I do. When you haven't got anything to say or anybody to talk to, just make a snobby face, like this." Signorina Niscemi sticks her nose in the air and pouts. "That way it looks like you don't want to talk to people because you think they're not quite your kind and you can't trust them."

Raffaella also sticks her nose in the air and pouts, then laughs.

"I told you we'd have a good time if you came," Signorina Niscemi says.

"I don't understand Signorina Niscemi," Rosy says to Cinzia and Alessia, sitting on the wicker couch on the other side of the garden. "You can see a mile off all she wants is somebody to eat her tits, so I don't know why the fuck she has to make that face!"

Tony is still thinking about Nunzio's impertinent answer and the missing amaretti when he sees Lou Sciortino and Leonard Trent coming in and his head starts spinning. Tony watches them for a moment, then walks toward them, but doesn't know where to start. "Cettina!" he screams. When he doesn't know what the fuck to do, he always screams, "Cettina!"

Cettina appears, holding the train of her red dress in her left hand and a glass of prosecco in her right. As she can't hold out her hand, she's forced to smile and bow. Lou smiles, while Leonard bows in reply.

"And this is Tony!" Tony says, pointing to himself, and looking at Leonard with a forced smile.

"*Ciao*, Tony," Leonard says, giving him his hand. "Nice party."

"Thank you," Tony says, holding out a hand as flabby as a fresh cuttlefish.

Then Tony falls silent, and so does Cettina. Lou is on the point of saying something stupid about how his jacket and Cettina's dress are both red, when Leonard looks straight in Agatino's direction.

"Marvelous!" he says.

"Who?" Tony asks in surprise.

"The octopus," Leonard says.

"The octopus?" Tony asks, even more surprised, remembering that in Sicilian, "octopus" can mean "faggot."

"Yes, the octopus . . . How do you say?" Leonard walks toward Agatino and, a few yards from the table where the aperitifs are, points to an octopus, made out of three feet of real pastry, with colored parasols stuck in its head and its tentacles used for holding glasses.

"Oh," Tony says, relieved. "Nice, isn't it? Almond pastry, like Uncle Sal's amaretti. Amazing what they can do with almond pastry!" Then he signals to Agatino. "An aperitif?"

Agatino puffs out his chest, wiggles his shoulders, and blinks behind the sunglasses. "A Bellini, a Rossini, or a Tonini?"

"A Tonini, please," Leonard says.

With the palm of his hand Tony indicates the anchovies and the raw octopus. "May I offer you some Sicilian sushi? Lou?"

"Thanks, Tony," Lou says, looking around. "Maybe I'll have something later."

"Mindy . . . is on her way," Cettina says timidly.

"Any chance of having a little of this . . . this . . . almond pastry?" Leonard says.

Tony turns white, looks at Cettina, and clears his throat. "The amaretti are on their way . . ." he says. "I know it's a shame, but we can't eat the octopus, can we?"

"Don't worry," Leonard says, smiling. "Sicilian sushi sounds perfect."

Tony cheers up, looks at Cettina like a contented child, then puts a hand on Leonard's shoulder. "Baretta . . ." he says in a shrill voice. "Is it true Baretta killed his wife?"

"No, thanks, not this octopus . . . just the other one." Leonard can't take his eyes off the octopus sculpture. "The lawyer says Marlon Brando's son Christian had an affair with his wife."

"The lawyer's wife?" Tony asks in a worried tone.

"No, Baretta's wife."

Tony jumps, like he's had a shock. "*Madre!*"

Leonard nods, then looks left and right. "But the whole defense doesn't add up."

Tony nods, too.

"Baretta and his wife were in a restaurant," Leonard goes on, "and they go out to the parking lot. But then, according to Baretta, he goes back to the restaurant because he forgot his gun. He goes in, gets the gun, and when he gets back to the parking lot, his wife's already been shot. Can you see somebody forgetting his gun in a restaurant?"

Tony shakes his head. "*Minchia*, they set him up! In my opinion, it was Marlon Brando's son. He already killed his stepsister's lover ten years ago because he was beating her—and that isn't normal, because you can kill your sister's lover, all right, but your stepsister's? If you kill your stepsister's lover, it means you're doing it because you have the hots for her . . ."

"Don't forget Duffy Hambleton, Tony, the stuntman who first accused Baretta of hiring him to kill his wife . . ."

"What the hell does Baretta got to do with Duffy's wife?"

"No, when I say his wife, I mean Baretta's wife . . ."

"Oh, yes . . ."

"Now he's changed his story and he's accusing Brando's son . . . There's also Kevin London, the parking lot mugger, Baretta's lawyer says it could have been him . . ."

Tony and Leonard Trent walk away, leaving Lou and Cettina to themselves.

In her right hand, Signora Zappulla clutches the fan her husband bought her in Córdoba and taps it nervously on the palm of her left hand. *Minchia*, Tony hardly even said good evening to her! *Asshole! Turncoat!*

A few yards away, Signora Falsaperla is reveling in the fact of Tony's treating the senator and his wife so badly. To Signora Falsaperla, who's arm in arm with her husband, his stomach barely contained by his red shirt with the mother-of-pearl buttons and his face aflame with aftershave, it seems too good to be true, seeing Signora Zappulla with her horse face contorted in rage, and hair like Farrah Fawcett in a wind tunnel. So she decides to unburden herself. "Signora," she says, approaching, "nice barbecue, isn't it? They've even got *americani* here."

"Let them go back to Hollywood and be ballbusters there. Then they can come here and act all high and mighty. By the way"— Signora Zappulla turns to Signor Falsaperla—"your wife told me at Tony's that you'd like to go into politics."

Signor Falsaperla's face gets even redder, because it's one thing to talk about having political ambitions when you're in your shop, wrapping sausages for your customers, and quite another in front of Senator Zappulla. But the senator tells him, "Excellent idea, excellent idea. The country needs entrepreneurs like you."

Nobody's ever called Falsaperla an entrepreneur before. His face almost explodes with happiness, and even the tips of his ears turn bright red.

"That's democracy, look!" Uncle Mimmo says to Tano, nudging him in the elbow and indicating Lou with his eyes.

"*Minchia*, that's the guy who came to collect the protection!" Tano says.

"Who?" Cosimo screams.

"Why don't you say it a little louder, eh?" Uncle Mimmo says. "He hasn't heard you yet."

During the afternoon Mindy called Valentina, took her into Tony and Cettina's bedroom, opened the wardrobe, and showed Valentina Tony's wife's clothes. Cettina had told her to choose something to wear and Mindy had thought, *Who better to decide than Valentina?* Among Cettina's things, Valentina immediately saw a simple seventies-style dress, white with blue polka dots, which seemed tailor-made for Mindy. Cettina's shorter, but just as big-breasted, and the dress fit her to a T, coming down to midthigh.

Valentina then rushed over to her own house and came back with a pair of stiletto-heeled sandals she bought on Via Etnea.

"When a woman's got beautiful feet like you do, Mindy, she oughta show them off," Valentina said as Mindy gazed in the mirror.

Now Mindy is advancing across the lawn, a surly expression on her face. She sways in an ungainly way as she walks, her white breasts shaking above the low-cut neckline.

"Mindy!" Cettina says, waving.

Mindy turns and sees Cettina with the *americano*, who's wearing an open red jacket.

Lou gives her a long, studied look as she approaches.

"Good evening," Mindy says when she's in front of Lou, keeping her knees together so she can plant her heels more firmly in the ground. Her voice is steady, and so are her eyes, which look straight into his.

Lou turns red and looks down.

"What are you doing, looking at my feet?" Mindy asks.

"What?" Lou says curtly.

Cettina smiles and gives Mindy a look that says, *You're gorgeous.* Then she signals to Agatino, who's moving among the guests with a tray full of the triad of aperitifs. Agatino approaches and whispers in her ear, "Signora, your husband's looking desperately for you."

"Are you having anything, kids?" Cettina says. "You'll have to excuse me. Apparently my husband's looking for me."

Mindy shifts her weight, trying to free her right heel, which is caught in the grass. "A Brancamenta," she says to Agatino with a slightly pained tone.

Fuck, Lou thinks, *just like my grandfather!*

She's spent years playing the saint, Agatino thinks, *and now look at the whore.*

"Make that two, please," Lou says, looking straight at Rosamunda, or Mindy, or whatever the fuck she's called.

Sì, principessa, ascoltami!
Tu che di gel sei cinta,
da tanta fiamma vinta,
l'amerai anche tu!

The voice of Violetta Leonardi, a soprano from the Teatro Massimo, rings out loud and clear, reaching every corner of the garden. It wasn't difficult for Senator Zappulla to get the soprano to grace Tony's barbecue, along with the tenor Pippo Del Gaudio, the two first violins, a cellist, and a pianist from the Massimo. They're performing a program of *chinoiserie et orientalisme*, according to Tony's instructions: mainly *Turandot* and *Butterfly* . . . *Tu che di gel sei cinta, Bimba dagli occhi pieni de malia, Un bel dì vedremo, Il cannone del porto, Tu, tu piccolo Iddio* . . .

The performance ought to have gone off without a hitch, but unfortunately Salvatore Attigliano, the first violin, grabbed all the amaretti for himself, and now he's having trouble keeping time.

Nick looks right and left, and then goes back and hides behind the garden gate. *Minchia*, opera, Americans, and Chinese dragons! All that's missing is for a coffin with Saint Agata's relics to pass by in procession.

Nick is terrified, because he's sure that as soon as he enters everybody will stop what they're doing and start applauding the fiancé's arrival.

Because it's one thing to take Mindy aside, although he's still not sure what she looks like because when they introduced her he felt faint, anyway it's one thing to take Mindy aside and say, "I'm sorry, Mindy, let's forget this." It's quite another thing to say to everybody, "Thanks a lot, but let's forget it" when her relatives are applauding you, the invitations are printed, the church is booked, the house is furnished, and Uncle Sal's as happy as could be.

As if that weren't enough, now he's got this fucking allergy to deal with! Never mind Uncle Sal, even Tony's plants bust your balls!

Nick is coughing and swearing at the top of his lungs when he becomes aware of a presence behind him. He turns abruptly and sees Valentina.

"Wipe your nose, it's running!" Valentina says, smiling, and hands him a Kleenex.

Tony approaches the girls on the wicker couch.

"Have you seen the amaretti?" he asks, in a sharp, angry voice.

"Huh?" Rosy says.

Tony folds his arms and drums with his foot.

"They gotta be here, Tony. There were trays of them," Alessia says.

"Oh, there were trays of them," Tony says, turning with legs apart and hands on hips and looking all around the barbecue. "Have you seen Cettina?" he asks, even more angrily.

Cinzia opens her eyes wide. "Fuck, Tony, you're firing off questions like a machine gun. We haven't seen her, but here's Nunzio, why don't you ask him?"

Tony glances down at the big rings of sweat under his armpits, swears, and grabs Nunzio's arm.

"Have you seen Cettina?"

"She was just talking to the *americano* and her cousin Mindy."

Shading his eyes with his hand, Tony looks around, and spots Lou talking to Mindy. No sign of Cettina.

"Listen, have you seen the amaretti?" Tony screws up his eyes very small.

"No. There was a box, but that was an hour ago."

"What do you mean . . . an hour ago? That director just asked me for amaretti. What am I going to give him, fried dicks?"

Nunzio smiles wickedly. "Maybe your wife hid them! Of course, if they don't turn up, you'll have to get more from Corso Italia!"

Minchia, Nunzio really loves stirring things up between Tony and his wife!

DON GIORGINO'S *ORZATA* IS
A RITUAL, A WAY OF SHOWING OFF

Don Giorgino's *orzata* is a ritual, a way of showing off. He used to buy it from the stands on Piazza Umberto when he was young. At the time he had torn pants, but there were lots of torn pants in those days. Your shoes, though, had to be good and shiny. And you kept the nail on your little finger really long to emphasize your ruby ring, because going to the stand in those days with the ring in clear view was like saying to everybody, *You're all dying of starvation, but I can afford an* orzata, *and when I buy it I've got a ring on my little finger, because Giorgino Favarotta isn't dying of starvation like all of you, and doesn't need to pawn things.*

He still has the same ring. A woman's ring, with a ruby, that he got from a pawnbroker. It used to belong to a baroness whose carob orchards had burned down in 1926 and who pawned the ring to pay for a dinner she was giving.

Now, though, Don Giorgino drinks his *orzata* at the Hollywood, a bar on Piazza Europa with small tables outside, where the local bad boys drive up in their convertibles at aperitif time. And where they keep *orzata* specially for him.

Don Giorgino arrives with a *picciotto*, sits down, leans on his cane, and remains still, looking behind his sunglasses at the hookers with their bare midriffs, while the *picciotto* orders for him.

You can either reach Piazza Europa from the seaside promenade, which is crowded with people coming back from the sea, or from Corso Italia, which crosses the city, and is deserted on Sunday, when all the shops are closed.

Pippino is coming from Corso Italia.

On foot, in his brown suit and black polo shirt. Walking fast and seeming resolute. To tell the truth, Pippino isn't the kind of guy who has to walk fast to seem resolute. Pippino doesn't even know what the fuck it means to be resolute. He was born that way and, like all men who are born a certain way, doesn't even know he is. Pippino is walking fast because he wants to be sweating when he arrives.

Fuck, how many hookers there are here, Don Giorgino is thinking as he waits for his *orzata. Look at them, plastic tits, fashionable shoes, they go to beauty salons, and they can't wait to suck the cocks of the guys in the convertibles!*

Don Giorgino bursts into a wild laugh. The *picciotto* sitting next to him doesn't turn a hair. Every now and again Giorgino starts laughing like a moron.

Pippino is walking with his head down. Faster than ever. He can feel the first beads of sweat dropping from his forehead. His stomach, though, is still dry.

When Pippino is tense, time slows down for him, and then he sees everything: he can see if a fly is passing close to your ear, if you've lied to your wife, if your feet are sweating in your shoes—everything. But when he relaxes, like now that he's walking fast, then time speeds up, and Pippino sees only what he wants to see and nothing else.

The waiter arrives with the *orzata*. Don Giorgino appears to be asleep. He's absolutely still, with his mouth half open, the tip of his tongue sticking out, and his breath coming out in a wheeze, rising from his throat. The waiter puts the glass down on a little silver dish in front of Don Giorgino.

Nothing for the *picciotto*. He's here to work, not drink coffee.

Don Giorgino, dozing off constantly, takes an hour to drink the *orzata*. His hand shakes and he sips his drink like a little bird. Every now and then he laughs . . . his usual wild laugh.

Pippino reaches Piazza Europa. He walks toward the Hollywood. He looks at the customers in the bar and spots Don Giorgino. As he approaches the table, he stumbles and overturns the *orzata*.

The waiter sees a man who's bathed in sweat apologizing to Don Giorgino, then putting his hand on the *picciotto*'s back and apologizing to him, too. The waiter comes running.

"I'm sorry, I'm sorry," Pippino's saying. "*Maria*, I'm sorry! Bring another one straightaway, the same thing, I'll pay, I'll pay, I'm sorry, I'm so sorry."

The young guys in the convertibles laugh, so do the hookers.

The waiter doesn't know what to do. He runs inside to order another *orzata* and to get a cloth to wipe the floor.

Pippino runs into the bar. "*Maria*, I'm so sorry . . . Give me a glass of water, please. *Maria*, I'm so sorry. Let me pay . . . What was it, an *orzata*? Please let me pay."

Pippino puts his hand in his pocket and takes out a wad of hundred-euro bills. Nancy, the cashier, who's wearing a white blouse with lace trimmings and has very big tits—quite obviously not the ones God gave her—looks him up and down: brown suit, long sleeves, wide trouser cuffs . . . a peasant in from some buttfuck village to chase after whores.

"Don't worry," she says, smiling.

"You must excuse me. *Maria*, I'm so sorry. Listen . . . is there a gas station open around here? My Mercedes broke down on Piazza Trento."

"Sure, there's a twenty-four-hour place on Piazza Trento, didn't you see it?"

"On Piazza Trento! *Maria*, I thought it was closed. It's Sunday. *Maria*, it's twenty-four hours. *Maria* . . . I'll be right back, okay?"

Pippino runs out. Nancy watches him, smiling.

"Hurry up," Nancy says to the waiter.

Nancy doesn't own the bar, she's just the cashier. But she likes telling the waiter to hurry up. Those who don't know often mistake her for the owner's wife.

The waiter has the tray with the *orzata* in one hand, and the bucket and cloth in the other. *Why don't you hurry up and suck my dick, whore?* he thinks. He places the *orzata* in front of Don Giorgino, picks up the remains of the broken glass from the ground, and starts to clean up.

"I'm sorry, Don Giorgino, I've got to clean it up now, before the flies get to it," he says.

The hookers and the young guys in the convertibles are still laughing, looking at the table.

The waiter wrings out the cloth inside the bucket. He notices Don Giorgino is bleeding from his nose. His mouth is half open, and the tip of his tongue is sticking out. *He's an old man, he shouldn't come out in this heat.* But it doesn't seem right to speak to

Don Giorgino with all that blood coming out of his nose. So he touches the *picciotto* on the shoulder, and the *picciotto* slowly drops his head until his forehead hits the table. The mother-of-pearl handle of a knife eight inches long is sticking out from under his armpit.

Pippino felt it when the knife touched the *picciotto*'s heart, just like he felt the soft bone on the bridge of the old man's nose yield abruptly. A trained hand is just like a knife that can think and feel.

Pippino goes down to the rocks below Piazza Europa. He takes off his shoes, his suit, and his polo shirt, and without a moment's hesitation dives into the water.

ettina, you're a disgrace to both houses!"

The barbecue is at its height and he expects to be understood without further explanation. Cettina tries to understand him. She really concentrates. Because when Cettina doesn't understand him, Tony loses his temper. And when Tony loses his temper, Cettina doesn't understand a fucking thing.

"What do you mean, both houses?" Cettina asks, while all around the barbecue is raging like a storm at sea.

Tony raises his eyes to heaven. "This one and your mother's, which you couldn't wait to get away from, that's why you married me . . . Where the fuck did you hide the amaretti?"

Cettina looks around. "What do you mean, where did I hide them? I didn't hide them!"

Tony sways. He raises his hands and moves his head from side to side.

Cettina gets frightened.

"So you're telling me you didn't hide the amaretti? You're informing me that all the amaretti in the house are already gone?"

Now he really is losing his temper! And when Tony loses his temper he acts like a puppet: he says something, rushes off, has second thoughts, comes back, curses, and rushes off again. It's like his strings are being pulled by an invisible demon.

Pippino is sitting on the rocks, smoking a cigarette, drying himself in the sun. The solarium on Piazza Europa has already been taken apart. There are two injured seagulls perched on the rocks, keeping him company.

Tony is sitting in his car, staring into space. When he got in, he slammed the door of the purple Fiat 127 hard, and the scented rubber flying saucer is still swaying on the rearview mirror. Tony had hurried across the ring road, looking right and left, raising his hands to stop the cars, even though there wasn't any fucking traffic. But Tony knows you shouldn't cross the ring road on foot, it's dangerous, that's why they built the elevated walkway.

Leaning on the blue plush steering wheel, he keeps repeating, "I can't believe it, I can't believe it, the amaretti all gone, the amaretti all gone . . ." Then he turns the key in the ignition and drives off, tires screeching.

Pippino stands up. He checks that his underpants are dry, looks at his watch, takes his pants off the rock, and puts them on, trying not to lose his balance.

At Scali's Amaretti, Nuccio is walking backward, bent ninety degrees, with his pants slipping down. He's dragging Uncle Sal by his feet around the second floor of the building, looking for a place to hide him. Uncle Sal seems deader than dead, because he's got a crossbow arrow in his neck, close to the jugular, but above all because he's letting himself be dragged without making any fuss.

Tony screeches to a halt at an angle on the sidewalk in front of the building on Corso Italia. He sits there for a couple of minutes, staring into space and shaking his head, then leans down to his right and looks for the key ring with the elephant and the obelisk. He finally gets out of the car, searching for the right key as he walks to the big brass and frosted glass door. On the glass there's a double S, the two letters intertwined.

Tony bends to put the key in the lock. He opens the door, goes in, walks quickly past Signorina Niscemi's desk, stops, turns back, looks right and left, goes closer to the desk, picks up a powder compact, opens it, smells it, smiles, grabs a bottle of nail polish, holds it up to the light, puts it down, picks up a nail file, looks at it a long time, then thinks about Signorina Niscemi's nails and throws it back on the desk.

Upstairs, Nuccio hears the sharp sound of the file being thrown on the desk. He stops, looks right and left, and straightens his pants.

Tony walks quickly toward the basement. He turns on the light and runs down the stairs. Boxes of amaretti in tall, tidy piles. He takes one, two, three . . . Then he takes a dozen boxes and, trying to hold them steady, turns and walks up the stairs. He switches off the light with his nose and, with short steps, heads for the door.

"Who are you?"

Startled, Tony drops the boxes. He turns and sees Nuccio.

"Nuccio . . ."

"Oh, Signor Tony."

What the fuck is Nuccio doing at Scali's Amaretti on a Sunday?

"Is Uncle Sal upstairs?"

"Who?" Nuccio comes slowly toward him.

What do you mean, who? You're here in my family's shop and you're asking who? Tony says nothing. He slowly retreats.

Nuccio keeps walking toward him. "Oh . . . Don Scali? Oh, yes . . . he'll be right back. He went to straighten something out and then he'll be right back."

He'll be right back. My uncle leaves you here all alone? You're putting me on! Tony keeps retreating. "All right . . . Tell him I needed some amaretti for my barbecue . . . Tell him . . ."

"When he gets here, I'll tell him . . ."

"I'll be going, then."

"Aren't you taking the amaretti?"

Tony looks at the amaretti.

Nuccio leaps on him all of a sudden and slams him down on Signorina Niscemi's desk.

Pippino arrives at Scali's Amaretti. He scans right and left along Corso Italia, then looks at the lock and sees the elephant key ring hanging from it. He takes out his knife and slips silently inside.

The scene that presents itself would scare anyone, but not him, not Pippino, Don Lou Sciortino's Oleander. On Signorina Niscemi's desk, Tony is sitting on top of Nuccio, pulling his hair with one hand, and with the other stabbing him repeatedly and screaming bloody murder. "No . . . Don't kill me . . . What did I do to you? . . . No . . . Please . . . I got a wife and kids . . . I got a wife and kids!"

Tony sees Pippino and stops.

Pippino goes closer.

Tony gets off Nuccio. He looks at Pippino's knife, then at the nail file he's holding in his own hand. He falls to his knees, all spattered with blood, and starts crying. "What did I ever do to you? I got nothing to do with this. Please . . . I beg you!"

Pippino leans over to look at Nuccio. He's dead.

He walks around Tony, without even deigning to look at him, and walks upstairs. He finds Uncle Sal lying motionless on the floor, his arms outstretched, an arrow stuck in his neck.

Pippino crouches and looks at the arrow.

What the fuck is this?

Then he stands up again, dusts down his pants, and goes downstairs.

Tony is still on his knees, begging God for mercy.

"Who the fuck are you?" Pippino asks.

"No, please, no . . . I only came to get some amaretti, amaretti . . . I don't got nothing to do with my uncle . . . I don't got nothing to do with it."

"Get up."

"Huh?"

"Get up. Let's go!"

"What?"

"I said let's go!"

Tony gets up. He looks at Nuccio lying dead as a doornail on Signorina Niscemi's desk and asks, "What is it? What happened?"

"Why did you kill your uncle?"

"What?"

Pippino looks at Nuccio. "Never mind. Let's go."

Tony doesn't understand anything anymore.

"The amaretti."

"What?"

"The amaretti. Didn't you come for the amaretti?"

Tony looks at the boxes. "Yes . . ."

"So take them."

Signora Lo Jacono's husband once came into Tony's salon. Tony greeted him and showed him where he could sit and wait while his wife was being taken care of. In response, Signor Lo Jacono punched him in the face, leaving him unconscious for fifteen minutes.

After that, he spent all afternoon sitting on the zebra-striped armchair, staring into space, while Agatino tried to shake him, screaming and swearing like somebody bitten by a tarantula.

Tony feels pretty much the same way now.

"In my opinion, you got nothing to do with this," Pippino is saying.

Bent over the wheel of the purple Fiat 127, Pippino drives slowly, taking care when he shifts gears because the car isn't his.

"In fact, in my opinion, nothing happened and you weren't even there."

Tony looks at him through half-closed eyes, a dumb expression on his face.

Pippino brakes so suddenly that the boxes of amaretti go flying. "Because otherwise, a year goes by, two years, ten years, I come looking for you, I find you and I kill you and that's it. Do we understand each other? You don't bother us, we won't bother you. Because otherwise I got to kill your wife, your kids, your nephews, and your aunts!"

Tony's dumb expression turns scared.

"What is this, some kind of stock car?" Pippino goes on. "*Minchia*, they don't make machines like this anymore! You know, I also got a license to drive cement mixers."

Pippino carefully puts the car in first gear and drives very slowly.

"Is this the way?" he asks, pulling up at an intersection.

"There . . . the rotary . . ." Tony whispers.

Pippino parks very carefully in front of Tony's garden. He gets out, straightens his jacket, and walks off the way he came. Tony watches him as he disappears along the ring road like Tony Baretta in the corridors of the New York subway.

"What happened? Who was that guy?"

Tony turns abruptly and sees Cettina leaning in at the window.

"Come on, did you get those fucking amaretti? Come on, hurry up, you got guests."

"Cettina," Tony whispers. "Will you do something for me? Will you get me a pair of pants and a shirt?"

"What, you going to change in the car?" Cettina says, looking right and left to see if anybody's watching.

"Cettina, please, let's don't get into an argument now, just get me a pair of pants and a shirt."

"All right, idiot. Just come inside with the amaretti, then go upstairs and change in the house."

"Cettina!" Tony screams.

Cettina walks to the house, gesturing angrily with her hands. "All right, I'm going, I'm going. *Minchia*, it's these fucking *americani*, they're making him nervous!"

When she returns with the pants and the shirt, Tony has a solemn expression on his face. "Sit down."

"In the car?"

"Sit down, I said." Tony is staring straight ahead of him.

"Okay, I'll sit down." Cettina walks around the car and sits down next to Tony. "Come on, now, what do you want?"

"They killed Uncle Sal," Tony says curtly.

Cettina opens her eyes and mouth wide and says nothing.

"Not long ago, at Scali's Amaretti."

"While you were there?" Cettina is scared.

Tony nods.

"And what did you do?"

"What did I do? I went in the stockroom, got the amaretti, came back upstairs, and there was Nuccio, trying to kill me!"

"Nuccio tried to kill you? Why? Did he kill Uncle Sal?" Cettina wriggles around on her seat.

"How the fuck do I know, Cettina, that's just the way it was!"

"And what did he do to you?"

"I don't know what he did. At some point this other guy came in, and after that, I don't know, Nuccio was dead, too."

"Dead? And who was the other guy?"

"The guy you saw just now. Cettina, if I tell you I don't know a fucking thing, it means I don't know a fucking thing. Look at me!" Tony shifts the boxes and shows Cettina his bloodstained shirt.

"What, you got hurt?" Cettina raises a hand to her mouth.

"No."

"Change right now!"

Tony makes a face, like he's saying, *What the fuck do you think I'm doing?*

"And the guy who killed Nuccio brought you home?" Cettina looks along the street.

"Yeah." Tony takes off his dirty pants.

"Why?"

"What do you want me to say?"

"Why didn't he kill you, too?"

"He said if he killed me, then he also had to kill you, and Rosy, and Alessia, and Mindy, and everybody. So he told me to keep my mouth shut, because if I don't keep my mouth shut, he'll come back and finish the job."

"But why did he bring you home?"

Tony stops and looks at his wife. "Why don't you go ask him, Cettina?"

Cettina bites her hands, then nods. That's the way Cettina is, she takes a while to be convinced.

"*Minchia*, I knew it was going to end up like this!"

"Cettina, I got to tell you something." Tony buckles his belt.

"Something else?"

"You know, it was me who killed Nuccio."

Cettina opens her eyes wide. "How?"

"How the fuck do I know?"

"What the fuck do you mean, how the fuck do you know?"

"Fuck, Cettina!"

"Fuck, Totó!"

Tony looks at his wife. It's been ages since she last called him Totó.

"He jumped me. What was I supposed to do?" Tony changes his shirt.

"And the other guy?"

"He came in later."

"And how did you kill him?"

"How the fuck do I know, Cettina? I don't even know if it was the other guy finished him off."

"I feel like I'm going to throw up, Tony!"

"Wait, this isn't the moment." Tony finishes buttoning his shirt. He looks in the glove box and takes out a cigarette. He lights it and looks out the window. "What do we do now?"

Cettina lifts her eyebrows. "What the fuck do you want to do? We always knew something like this would happen to Uncle Sal sooner or later . . ."

Tony blows the smoke out the window.

"Listen to me," Cettina says, looking him in the eyes. "We're good people, and they know that. The reason you're alive is because it's not in their interest to make things more complicated than they already are. And if it's not in their interest, it's not in ours, either. I was born poor, you know, and you've been cutting hair for ages. Is it our fault your uncle got mixed up with certain people?"

Tony looks out the window again.

"What are you doing, crying?"

"No," Tony says, without turning around.

"Right now our garden is full of *americani*, beautiful people from the movies who don't know a fucking thing about any of this shit. You know? There's even a photographer from *La Sicilia* here, they want to do an article."

Tony looks at Cettina out of the corner of his eye.

"Mindy's getting it together with that guy. Valentina's walking Nick all around, showing him pictures of when she was little."

Tony gives a melancholy little smile.

"And now you want to ruin the lives of all these people who don't know anything? Why? Think about it, Tony! You're the head of the family. You got a responsibility." Cettina starts stroking his hair. "That guy who was here is gone. What do we know about these things? These guys grab each other, kill each other, make wars! We're good people. One of these Sundays we should go to church. Eh, Tony, how about it?"

Tony nods, still looking out the window. "The guy said I had nothing to do with it . . ."

"Maybe it was him, Tony. Just think about it. Excuse me, but I saw him bringing you home. Whaddaya think, somebody who goes into Scali's Amaretti on a Sunday is there to buy amaretti? Tony, the guy was right. You don't got nothing to do with it. Now, are you going to do something?"

"What?" Tony asks, rubbing his eyes.

"Let's get out of this car and go to our barbecue. The guests are waiting. Just imagine if they killed Uncle Sal ten years ago. Remember the time they tried to ambush him at the tollgate on the autostrada?"

"He said . . . he said they had the wrong person," Tony says, sniffling.

"Tony . . ." Cettina says, still stroking his hair.

Tony looks at his wife and nods.

Cettina continues stroking his hair.

"Tony . . ."

"Cettina . . . I love you . . ."

"Totó . . ." Cettina says, pulling him to her and half closing her eyes.

"Fuck," Tony says, "you're right. Let's go!"

Tony hurries out of the purple Fiat 127 without even closing the door. Cettina stays for a moment with her hand in midair, then she smooths the skirt of her red dress, straightens the train, gets out of the car, looks at the garden, and slams the car door so hard the flying saucer on the rearview mirror finally takes flight.

AT MARZAMEMI, THE SEA TODAY
IS LIKE A SHEET OF GLASS

At Marzamemi, the sea today is like a sheet of glass, and Brancati's island seems to be lying on it. It's still hot, but in the shade of Don Mimmo's veranda the wind feels cool.

Don Mimmo is walking along the boardwalk and his steps echo in the silence. The only table that's been laid is Don Lou's. The other three are empty and haven't even got tablecloths. There are no more foreigners, and Don Mimmo has stopped putting the red checkered oilcloths on the tables, because the wind would blow them away.

Pippino is getting dressed on the beach. He swam all the way to the island and back while Don Mimmo was making the sauce for the *spaghetti alla pescatora*. Don Lou could even hear the sound of his strokes.

He's sitting with his back to the reinforced concrete scaffolding because he doesn't want to see it, and he's drinking red wine. When Pippino comes back from his swim and sits down opposite him,

Don Lou says, "It's concrete, Pippino, just concrete. All you need is a bomb . . ."

Pippino thinks about this, then tucks his napkin in his shirt collar, looks down, and nods.

Fuck, Don Lou thinks, *whatever happened to the good peasants and the assholes we used to have, the generous noblemen and the grumpy ones, the men of honor and the ones who screwed up? What happened to the time when all you needed was a ring on your little finger and being able to talk like the men of honor talked, saying some things and keeping quiet about others, even if what you were saying or keeping quiet about didn't mean a fucking thing? And the Festival of San Sebastiano, the ricotta in the pot, the pruning of the carob trees and the holes in the ground for the charcoal, the olives roasting on the grill, the shiny shoes and the noblemen's clubs, the lowered eyes and the boys with ropes for belts, the duels with knives and the onion salad, the carnival with the fairground booths and the games of chance, the heat you couldn't get away from, the lemon water, the lazy afternoons and the women who threw themselves on the bed, the black hair and blue eyes, the brilliantine and the short ties, the puppet shows and the singers who told stories with their songs, the men who shook the trees and the women who gathered what fell, the hunger and the charity, the sun and the anger, the dignity and the respect, the "May I kiss your hand?" and the "God bless Your Honor," the workingmen's clubs and the secret societies, the brigands, the priests with guns, the brokers and matchmakers, the cutthroats, the bottle of perfume, the jasmine in a drawer, the black brassieres, the afternoon siesta and the whole village waking up in the evening, the variety shows and the dancers, the contracts and the death sentences, the word that was sacred and the kissing of the cross, the pinstripe suits, the cuff links, the box at the opera house in Catania, where are they all? Where are all those stupid things that were so much a part of life, where are the friends who supported you?*

"Taste this. It's wine from Pachino. It's good for you." Pippino pours Don Lou another glass.

"Eh?"

"Taste it. It's wine from Pachino," Pippino repeats.

Don Lou isn't crazy about wine from Pachino, but he drinks it, because a Sicilian's got to drink wine from Pachino.

"Now we're going back," Don Lou says, "we got to start thinking about the La Brunas. I'm not leaving Starship Pictures in their hands!"

Pippino nods.

"What do you think about my grandson, Pippino?"

Pippino looks at Brancati's island. "I think whatever you think. It's hard for me to say, he's so quiet."

Don Lou nods. "He had this thing when he was small, whenever he did something bad, he used to stand in front of the stove, looking all innocent. Do you think he did all this on purpose?"

"Maybe he wanted to see his grandpa behave the way he did in the old days."

"Let's order," Don Lou says.

Pippino signals to Don Mimmo.

Don Mimmo approaches, walking unsteadily.

"Sit down, Don Mimmo," Don Lou says. "You're getting old, too."

Don Mimmo takes a chair, brushes the sand off it with the tablecloth, and sits down.

"You remember the old days, Don Mimmo?"

Don Mimmo smiles. "What old days, Don Lou?"

"Precisely," Don Lou says. "Do me a favor, Pippino. If anything happens to me in America, take my grandson aside and tell him the old days never existed, we used to stumble along then just like we do now. Tell him things are the same now as they always were, the Sicily I told him about exists only in my head. Tell him there were never rules and laws, honor and dignity, justice and secret societies. Tell him, tell my grandson all the things I told him about are still to come."

EPILOGUE

In the purple Fiat 127, Tony beats the blue plush steering wheel in time to the music from the CD. When Shocking Blue launch into the chorus, Tony and Agatino share the task. "I'm your Venus," Tony sings.

"I'm your fire at your desire," Agatino follows him.

Tony is driving slowly. Sitting behind him, you notice that all the people speeding by on the left are turning to look at you.

After three Brancamentas and a couple of gin and tonics at the barbecue, Mindy said, "Shall we go?"

"Go where?" you asked.

"To Acitrezza," she said. She was swaying, and she dug her heels even deeper into the grass to keep still. "It's a magical place. You can still see the stones the cyclops threw at Ulysses when he was blinded!"

———

Tony's wife stammered something incomprehensible when you said goodbye to her. The two of you took a taxi to Acitrezza, and on the seawall you stopped at a stand. To reduce your intake, you drank a seltzer with lemon and salt. Disgusting! Your head started turning, and instinctively you leaned on her, brushing against her right side and a bit of her ass. She laughed like a little girl, hit you on the head with her handbag, and started running. After a few yards, she stopped, with her red heel in her hand. Still laughing, she took off both sandals and walked barefoot along the seafront. You bought a phosphorescent plastic ball from a Chinese woman. A boy shouted at her, "Eh, *americana!*" and whistled with the thumb and index finger of his right hand in his mouth. She said, "*Americana*, my ass!" and put the little finger of her right hand in her mouth and gave a very sharp, very loud whistle. In front of the Church of San Giovanni Battista she ran quickly up and down the steps a couple of times. It made you think maybe she was crazy. You sat down at a bar on the seafront and knocked back another couple of gin and tonics. You went to the fish market and bought a tuna at four o'clock in the morning. With the wrapped-up tuna under your left arm, you emptied your right pocket at the desk of the hotel, which naturally was called the Odyssey, looking for your ID card. When you got to the room, she went right to the bathroom, still laughing, and you lay down on the bed. In a few minutes, you were fast asleep.

When you woke up, she was asleep, lying on her back. Her white blouse had ridden up her stomach, so you could see her panties, white with a raised edge. She was sleeping with her legs together, the panties wadded between them. She had very white skin and an ass so round her back wasn't completely flat on the sheet. You put your left hand between her legs and heard a kind of moan and then nothing. With your little finger and ring finger you lifted her panties and slid your hand underneath. She opened her eyes, put her legs to-gether even more, and turned to you with her mouth open.

"In Sicily, Lou, there comes a time when you're nothing but a brain and a dick, *capish*? It's like your stomach disappears." During the days you spent in that room, you thought about your grand-father several times.

This morning the sun entered the room like a slap in the face. When the phone rang, you thought it was noon and the guy in reception wanted to tell you the boy was coming up with a late breakfast. In-stead, the guy was stammering in a mixture of Italian and English.

"Sir, a *signore* . . . *diciamo* . . . a *signore* . . . is waiting for you."

"Where is he?" you asked.

"In the lobby, sir."

Mindy was still asleep. You ran downstairs, tucking your shirt into your jeans on the stairs as best you could. At the foot of the stairs, you saw Agatino, completely dressed in black, black suit, black shirt, with a bracelet of blue stones on his right wrist.

Agatino saw you, then half closed his eyes, lifted his head with a pout, crossed his hands on his lap, wiggled his shoulders, and said, "Signor Tony is waiting for you in the car."

In the room, you woke Mindy and told her. As you both gathered your things, the red jacket, the underwear, you asked her if she'd spoken to anybody in the last few days.

"No," she said.

At that moment, you realized for the first time what was going on: you'd run away with the girl, fucked her, and now you had to marry her! This was how people got married in this fucking country!

Tony was standing in front of the purple Fiat 127. He, too, was dressed all in black. "Get in!" he said solemnly, opening the door. You sat down in the backseat with Mindy. Mindy was silent, her head slightly bowed. Your hands were sweating.

"Where are we going?" you asked in a hoarse voice.

"To Uncle Sal's," Tony said, starting the car. "He's waiting for us in church."

Fuck you, you thought, *fucking men of honor! Fuck you, you fucking people who never talk clearly! Fuck you, too, Grandpa! Fuck you, puppet shows, seltzer with lemon and salt, and amaretti, "May I kiss your hand?" and "God bless Your Honor"! Fuck you, fucking sun! Fuck you, dignity and respect! Fuck you, Italy, fuck you!*

"What do you think, Agatino?" Tony said, after a few minutes' silence. "Maybe he should take off the red jacket!"

Agatino was sitting in the front next to Tony, looking through Tony's CDs. "The Queen Mother of England wore a red suit at the ceremony for her dead groom."

"But he's not the Queen Mother! On a man, red doesn't look right for a funeral!"

"A funeral? What funeral?" you asked.

Tony turned. He was smiling.

"Uncle Sal's funeral," he said. "While the barbecue was going on, they killed him at Scali's Amaretti with an arrow from a crossbow . . . Nuccio died, too!" Modestly, Tony didn't say how Nuccio had died.

Fuck, you thought, *Pippino killed everybody with Uncle Mimmo's crossbow!*

———

After exactly a minute of silence, Mindy started laughing, softly at first, then unrestrainedly. Almost immediately the laughter infected Agatino. As he laughed, he kept repeating, "With an arrow! *Minchia!*" Tony laughed, too. At one point, he was laughing so hard it almost sounded like he was wheezing. "*Minchia*, Agatino," he said, punching the steering wheel, "put on a CD! Life goes on!"

Agatino didn't need to be asked twice, he already had a seventies compilation in his hand, he pulled out the player, put in the CD, and was already swaying before the music even started.

Now you're all singing together at the top of your lungs.

I'm your Venus, I'm your fire at your desire!

ACKNOWLEDGMENTS

Thanks to I know who.